SOMETHING NEW &

Friends & Moore Series

CELESTE GRANGER

ACKNOWLEDGEMENT

Here we are again! I love the Moore family. All the girls are special in their own way. They are not perfect, they have flaws, but don't we all? And the men? Whew! Swoon worthy! I decided that some of the friends of the Moore family deserve a real chance at mind blowing, heart pounding love, too. Don't you agree?

Thank you so much for your support. I am truly humbled and grateful that you have been willing to take a chance on little ole me 😊 Your cheers of support, reviews and words of encouragement bolster my desire to write great stories that you will come to know and love. Thank you! <3

I also want to thank my graphic designer, Alpha reader, editor and literary support team. You guys work behind the scenes to help bring it all together and I appreciate you. Thank you to my friends and family who put up with me, understand when I am stuck in front of my computer, and love me anyway... lol

This book is dedicated to all those who can appreciate unexpected love...

"With the exchange of vows and the giving and receiving of rings, we've come to the part of the ceremony I know you've been waiting for Lance."

Lance smiled, and laughter spread from guest to guest.

"Samantha, Lance, I now pronounce you husband and wife. You may now kiss your bride!"

Lynette's heart was full as she watched her best friend Samantha, marry the man of her dreams. Lynette Jones was intimately familiar with the challenges Samantha faced in finding true love. She and Samantha worked together in the mailroom of Preston Industries when Samantha was single and struggling. Lynette witnessed firsthand, the beginning and manifestation of Sam's relationship and how it had come full circle. Yet, despite all the struggles, the doubt, the lingering questions, Sam pushed through and now, she was Mrs. Lance Preston. Lynette dabbed the tears that effortlessly spilled from her eyes. She couldn't help it. Sam was like family to her, and to see her bestie so happy genuinely warmed Lynette's heart. She was so enamored with the ceremony and all the love that was being shared, Lynette didn't notice the man who couldn't stop staring at her.

Although Samantha and Lance had an intimate wedding ceremony with family and a few friends, the reception held a week later on New Year's Eve was open to the couples extended circle. The exquisite Chateau Elan was the location of the reception. Chateau Elan was like a fairytale castle, nestled amidst 3500 acres of land encompassing sixty-three holes of championship golf, acres of vineyards for the private stock wine collection, European style spas, Olympic size pools and a thirty-five thousand square foot mansion where the "All That Glitters" reception was being held in the Paris Ballroom. As requested, all the guests were decked out in either silver or gold in honor of the reception theme. The Moore family was fully represented, including the elder women, Mary Elizabeth and Big Mama, otherwise known as Margaret. Although Lance hired renowned wedding planners for the reception, Lynette took her maid of honor duties seriously. She still felt the need to ensure everything was perfect for her best friend.

The Paris Ballroom was stunning with golden dupioni silk drapes cascading from five tier chandeliers dotting the ceiling. The round tables for the guests were covered intermittently in gold or silver tablecloths with crystal vases holding flowers and candles that reflected the beautiful shimmering colors in the room. The chairs the guests sat in were translucent, offering no visual obscurity to the room's fine décor. In the center was a dance floor with the couple's initials highlighted in black against a silver and gold semi-opaque backdrop. Balancing on four-inch silver stilettoes, Lynette flitted through the large ball-room making sure that the presentation to the guests was perfect. She also attended to Samantha, making sure the bride had everything she needed.

"Lyn, come on, relax," Samantha encouraged as Lynette approached the head table. "You've done a wonderful job."

"Thank you, sis," Lynette replied with a smile. "I just have a few more things I want to check on and the I'll relax."

"Well, make sure you are back in time for the bouquet

toss," Samantha replied. "We'll be doing that in just a few minutes."

"I'll be there, but I'm not sure why," Lynette giggled. I've caught the bouquet before and... nothing!" Lynette lifted her left hand to show the absence of a wedding ring.

Samantha leaned over with a slithering smile on her lips.

"Be there, ma'am," the bride insisted.

"Fine," Lynette snapped back. "I will."

As Lynette sashayed away, his eyes tracked her across the room. And when she momentarily fell from view, Elijah Sinclair, shifted his six-foot three-inch frame enough to bring her back into full view. His eyes narrowed as he watched her, and Elijah unconsciously folded in his bottom lip as he watched the seductive sway of her lips and the length of her sexy legs navigate through the space. Multimillionaire, Elijah Sinclair, architect extraordinaire, was responsible for some of the most famous buildings and homes around the world. His distinct design aesthetic is what first drew Lance Preston's attention. The two met a few years ago when Elijah was commissioned by Preston Industries to design their newest facility in southern California. Since then, Elijah designed the home Lance and Samantha currently reside in. The men became not only business associates but good friends. Elijah was here as a guest of Lance's. Elijah smiled to himself as he continued to watch Lynette, waiting for his opportunity to approach her. She'd caught his attention a few times before when he visited Preston Industries. Elijah never said anything to Lynette. It never seemed to be the right time. This? This was his chance. He would have to make a point to thank Lance later.

"Excuse me," Elijah offered as he began to move across the room. The depth of his baritone voice drew the unfiltered attention of every woman who heard him, and a smile from the ones he actually spoke to. Many feminine eyes trailed his athletic frame as he glided across the ballroom floor. Elijah had waited as long as he could to finally make his move. Watching her was satisfying, true enough, but he refused to settle for that. He wanted to talk to Lynette and determine if she was just as alluring in person. Elijah fully expected she would be, as he adjusted the Hermes Suave bowtie he wore and ran his large hands across the front of his Stefano Ricci custom tuxedo jacket. Elijah wanted Lynette's first impression of him to be memorable; no distractions from a crooked tie or wrinkled suit.

As Lynette came into view, Elijah cleared his throat, making sure to keep his eyes on her. He didn't want to lose her again among the bustling crowd. Elijah could feel the escalation of his beating heart pounding in his chest. He stood immediately behind her, watching Lynette fiddling with the guest gift baskets for when the reception was over.

"Excuse me, Ms. Jones?"

Lynette heard the thick rumble of a voice behind her.

"Ye- "

The word seemed to stick in her throat as she twirled around in response; her eyes met with an expansive chest. Whoever it was stood close enough for Lynette to inhale a scent of his cologne. Slowly, Lynette's eyes trailed down. It was a habit, spawn from conversations she had with her grandmother. *You can tell a lot about a man by what he wears on his feet.* Although Lynette wasn't much for labels, the Tom Ford Alligator cap loafers the man wore screamed that he took great care of his feet. Lynette's mink lashes fluttered as she traced his length, taking in the way his tailored slacks hung and the cut of his jacket. Just past his bow tie, Lynette took special note of the perfect trim of his beard that seamlessly connected to a trimmed mustache surrounding his mesmerizing lips. Her eyes drank in the smoothness of his dark chocolate skin without missing the strength of his refined nose. When her almond shaped eyes finally met his, Elijah found he couldn't immediately speak. She was breathtaking.

4

They stared into each other's eyes, both feeling as though time stopped for such a moment as this. Elijah shook himself from the momentary stupor he was in and cleared his throat again.

"Hi there, I'm Elijah."

An easy unfiltered smile moved across his lips that entranced Lynette. She didn't even notice his extended hand waiting to receive hers.

"Oh, hi," she finally replied. "I'm Lynette." She was able to draw herself from his perfect smile and accept the hand offered to her. "But somehow I get the feeling you know that already."

His reverberating laugh was interrupted by the crack of the microphone in the main room.

"Ladies! It's time for the tossing of the bouquet! All single ladies, please make your way to the dance floor!"

"I'm so sorry," Lynette uttered as her eyes moved from Elijah towards the dance floor. "I promised the bride."

Elijah didn't get a chance to explain that yes, he knew her name. He didn't even get a chance to say he understood why she had to go. Before he could say anything, Lynette eased her hand from his and started toward the dance floor. Although slightly disappointed, Elijah smiled as he turned and watched Lynette join the group of eligible women in the center of the dance floor.

IF I HAVE MY WAY, she'll never do that again, Elijah thought. His brows furrowed as his inner conversation caught him off guard. He didn't even know her, and had only spent a few stolen moments with her, Elijah consciously thought. How could he make such a declaration?

The mood around the bouquet toss was high. Many of the guests stood around watching and cheering. The women on the floor anticipated the tossing of the bouquet. Catching it meant that their dreams of wedded bliss could really come true; or so the old wives tale suggested. Lance, being the perfect gentleman, escorted Samantha to the dance-floor. When he planted a heated kiss on her lips, the crowd roared in approval. Samantha looked incredible in a platinum and gold calf length evening dress that hugged her curvaceous figure in all the right places. Lance was dapper in his black custom designed tux with bowtie and pocket square that perfectly matched Samantha's ensemble. Sam still wore that bridal glow as she separated from her husband and turned to face the eager singles.

"Ladies, are you ready?" Samantha asked, lifting the simulated bouquet overhead.

There was a collective, "yes", that poured from the women on the dancefloor. Samantha's eyes scanned the crowd, looking for her best friend. Of course, Samantha intended to play fair in tossing the flowers, but if she could get the bouquet in the general direction of her bestie, that would be fate, right? Lynette deserved love and Samantha desperately wanted that for her friend. No harm in tempting fate, she thought as her eyes trailed the smiling faces of the women staring at her. She didn't see Lynette though, even after lifting onto her tiptoes and eyeing the group again. But Samantha knew she couldn't delay any longer. If it was meant to be, Lynette would end up with the bouquet.

With a smile, Samantha spun on her five-inch, platinum Christian Louboutin's, turning her back to the excited crowd. Lynette stood in the furthest corner of the crowd. She smiled, but far less enthusiastically than the women around her. She didn't want to get her hopes up unnecessarily. At the same time, she did promise Samantha she would participate.

"Let's count it down, ladies, from three," the announcer suggested.

After the announcer said, 'three', the entire body of guests joined in.

"Two, one!"

As the group yelled one, Samantha released the bouquet with a dramatic overhead swing. She twirled around again, wanting to see who the recipient of bridal good fortune would be.

"Yay! Oh my God!" A woman who caught the bouquet exclaimed excitedly. Samantha smiled and clapped with everyone else in the room, still, combing the group looking for Lynette. Samantha's bestie clapped as well as she quietly stepped away from the dancefloor and faded to the background. But she wasn't invisible, not to Elijah. While everyone was gathering, Elijah made his way back into the ballroom. He kept his eyes on Lynette and watched her go through the motions. Elijah wondered why she wasn't excited about the prospect of catching the bouquet. He intended to find out.

Elijah strolled across the carpeted floor and positioned himself close to Lynette. He didn't say anything, just stood next to her. Lynette was preoccupied with the activities of the people still on the dancefloor. She didn't see Elijah approaching in her periphery. However, it didn't take Lynette long to sense his presence. She instinctively lowered her head and smiled when she recognized his distinct footwear. Realizing it was him, Lynette's heart started beating a little faster and suddenly she was conscientious of her posture. Crossing her legs at her ankles, Lynette lifted her head and stood up straight, making sure to keep her eyes forward as if she hadn't noticed.

"You didn't want to catch the bouquet?"

Eww, lawd that voice, Lynette quivered as Elijah's reverberating voice moved through her. He leaned in, closing the distance between them and whispered close to her ear. He was too close for Lynette to be able to concentrate on what he said. She tightened her thighs, bracing, as the quivering continued to her core. Elijah smiled as he watched Lynette trying to avoid looking in his direction. He was tempted to reach out, gently place his fingers under her delicate chin, and turn her in his direction. But Elijah resisted the urge. He didn't want her to think him too forward. Lynette gathered herself enough to respond to Elijah's inquiry.

She had to turn in his direction, so he could hear her over the crowd. When she did, their lips were close; a whisper away from connecting. Elijah didn't turn his head on his own. Lynette smiled and shook her head, reaching up with her hand and gently touching the side of his chin so she could access his ear.

Lynette touched him. Elijah felt her gentleness in his soul. His eyes closed slowly and opened, more hooded than they were before. Lifting onto her tiptoes, Lynette cupped her hand and spoke into his diamond-studded ear.

"Been there done that," Lynette whispered.

As she lowered herself, Elijah extended a hand to the small of her back. It was instinct. Lynette didn't flinch from his touch. She felt the strength of him. When Elijah said something else, Lynette could barely hear him.

"Say that again," she replied, doing her best to speak over the noise while still remaining lady-like.

Elijah got the message and gainer her eyes, gesturing that they step out of the main room. Lynette nodded, reading his gesture, and the touch of the hand to the small of her back increased as Elijah guided them to the periphery of the group and then out into the hallway. The duo continued to walk together until the sounds from the ballroom faded to near nothingness.

"I'm sorry," Lynette offered. "It was so hard to hear in there."

"Never apologize for something you have no control over, beautiful," Elijah crooned.

"Okaaay," Lynette answered. She couldn't help but smile. There was something about Elijah that put her at ease and made her smile. When Elijah extended his hand, offering Lyn a seat on the cushioned bench in the hall, she accepted. Elijah waited until Lynette was comfortably seated before sitting down next to her. He was careful not to crowd her space, but also careful to incline himself in her direction so they could talk face to face. Lynette felt a whirling in her belly and a pounding in her chest. She took a deep breath, exhaling slowly. She didn't want to let Elijah see the kind of affect he had on her. Besides, this man was practically a stranger.

"I never did get a chance to ask, but how did you know my name; and not just my first name but my government name," Lynette asked.

Elijah laughed as he stroked his beard. Lynette pursed her lips and slightly rolled her neck, waiting for a reply.

"I'm friends with the groom," Elijah explained. "I may have made an inquiry."

"About me?" Lynette asked, her hand moving to cover her heart.

"I hope that's not too unsettling for you," Elijah began.

"I haven't decided yet," Lynette quipped.

Elijah smiled. She was feisty and quick-witted. He liked that.

"What will help you decide," Elijah inquired, still wearing a brooding smile.

"Depends," Lynette purred. "What are your intentions?"

"Only good, I promise," Elijah trilled, taking a thick finger and crossing his heart. "It's just, when I see someone that intrigues me, I have to do my due diligence."

"So, what else did you find out about me," Lynette asked as she folded her arms across her chest.

"All I wanted was your name," Elijah explained. "I wanted to learn the rest for myself, firsthand."

Lynette tightened her eyes as she tried to determine the truth of what Elijah said. His closed lip smile was sexy as hell, but Lynette refused to be distracted by his swagger.

"Why though," Lynette asked. She was curious. She was skeptical. Her history with men made it so. Everything about Elijah screamed masculine, sexy alpha male. The clothes he wore screamed money, and a second look at his left hand screamed sexy ass eligible bachelor. Elijah watched as Lynette's eyes trailed to his wedding finger. When she looked up, he captured her eyes with a deep penetrating gaze.

"Because, you intrigue me, and I wanted the chance to get to know you." Elijah crooned. "Will you give me a chance?"

Lynette's pouty lips relaxed a little, but her eyes stayed narrow as she continued to evaluate his proposal. She was in disbelief; someone like Elijah showing interest in her.

"I don't even know your last name," Lynette playfully sassed.

"Sinclair," Elijah replied. "Elijah Sinclair."

T he bride and groom took to the dance floor. Lance held Samantha with such loving conviction, staring into her eyes and ignoring the rest of the world that every hopeless romantic in the room swooned. He made it so easy to be swept up in his aura, it was so strong, powerful and overwhelming. But Sam knew Lance's strength was all about her covering; protecting her from dangers seen and unseen, covering her heart with his intoxicating love, and being her best friend, on top of everything else. Samantha smiled against Lance's full lips as he swept her up in his arms, twirling her until her feet barely touched the ground.

"I love you, baby," Lance crooned against Samantha's succulent lips.

"I love you more," Samantha answered back.

"Impossible," Lance insisted with a burning kiss to her lips.

Samantha laced her arms around Lance's neck and pulled him in close. As the announcer invited others to join the bridal couple on the dance floor, Samantha whispered in Lance's ear.

"Have you seen Lyn?"

"No, I haven't, gorgeous," Lance replied. "I've been a little preoccupied."

"As you should be," Samantha purred. As the two separated when an upbeat song came on, Samantha scanned the room in search of her best friend. When she turned her attention back to her husband, Lance was wearing a slick smile.

"What is that about," Samantha cooed, finding herself smiling because of his smile.

"Lynette may be a little preoccupied as well," Lance trilled.

"And what do you know about that," Samantha asked, genuinely intrigued.

"Maybe just a little something," Lance replied.

"Tell me! What?" Samantha demanded.

"Not what," Lance responded, leaning in to make sure she heard him. "It's who?"

Samantha's eyes brightened as she saw how sneakily her husband was looking.

"Who is it, Lance? Tell me!"

"Elijah Sinclair," Lance hummed.

"Oh my God! Bae! That would be so awesome," Samantha chimed.

"I'm glad you approve," Lance answered, pulling his wife in close to him.

"I definitely do."

The smile remained on Samantha's face as she and lance danced to some of her favorite R&B tunes. Samantha wanted for her friend what she was blessed enough to find for herself. And Lynette deserved all the love the universe had to offer. Lynette was selfless, hardworking, and a great friend. She was a romantic at heart; yet, the men that Lynette dealt with never lived up to her expectation of what real love looked like. She gave more than she received. She loved harder than they deserved. Samantha closed her eyes and kissed Lance sweetly on the neck. She thanked him and sent beams of positive energy Lynette's way.

"WELL MR. SINCLAIR, maybe it's the holiday spirit or all the romance in the air, or maybe I'm just crazy, but for some reason that still escapes me, I'm willing to take that chance." Lynette's smile was sheepish as she spoke. She was honest though. Normally, she kept her guard up, unwilling to expose herself because she had been so disappointed in the past by the choices she made. But, for some reason, she didn't feel the need to be as guarded with Elijah. His aura put her in a place where she was unexpectedly comfortable. That should have made Lynette wary. She'd exposed herself before only to be let down. She hoped she wasn't making a mistake again.

"Well, Lynette, whatever the reason, I appreciate your willingness," Elijah began. "And I promise my intentions are honorable."

"I'm gonna hold you to that," Lynette cooed.

"Please do."

Heat rose in Lynette's cheeks again as his eyes found her and held her captive. There was a tumbling in her stomach and she absentmindedly placed her hand there, doing her best to settle her flighty emotions. This time though, Elijah did what he wanted to do before. Gingerly, he placed two fingers under her delicate chin and eased her attention back towards him. The fluttering in her belly escalated from such a simple touch. When Lynette lifted her eyes to meet his, she lost herself there in the depths of his gaze. Lynette wasn't sure what she was searching for, but what she found was that the tightness in her chest started to relax. The butterflies continued to cartwheel in her stomach, but it no longer made her feel like she had to self-sooth. There was a calm in his dark brooding eyes, balanced against the raciness of the slight smile on his lips.

"Will you walk with me," Elijah asked without dropping his eyes from imprisoning hers.

"Yes," Lynette murmured.

She watched as Elijah lifted his tall frame to standing and then extended his hand to assist her. Lynette didn't hesitate to fold her hand into his and feel the strength of him as he helped her up. It didn't take long before they fell in sync, step for step, although his gait was longer than Lynette's five-foot seven frame could manage. Elijah accounted for that. he didn't want to walk ahead of her. He wanted to walk beside Lynette, so he shortened his stride, so she didn't feel the need to rush her natural sway. It might have been a little thing, but it was something Lynette noticed. Relationship history and past failings taught her to take note of the small things, even more than the grand gestures. It was in the little details that you learned the soul of a man.

The duos leisurely stroll took them through the heart of the chateau. The castle-like atmosphere was resplendent with luxurious décor, yet there was a comfortable, cozy feeling in the expansive rooms.

"So, tell me Mr. Sinclair, how do you know Lance?"

"We've done some business together," Elijah replied.

There was something about Lynette's caramel skin, full lips, and dimpled cheeks that continued to draw his gaze. Her auburn hair was pulled away from her face, showing off Lynette's high cheek bones and elegant, swan like neck. If she was wearing any makeup at all, it was barely detectable, allowing her natural beauty to shine through. But Elijah knew, even from a distance, that she was more than just her looks. There was something in her eyes that said she was compassionate. There was something in her laugh, that said she loved life, and there was something in they way she carried herself that said she was strong despite everything the world had thrown at her. Elijah wanted to know everything he didn't know about her and so much more. He was hungry for her.

"What kind of work do you do, may I ask," Lynette asked as she sauntered beside him.

"I'm an architect," Elijah replied. He really hated talking about himself. Regardless of how accomplished he was, Elijah was humble and not the least bit braggadocious. Elijah would rather talk about anything other than himself, but he understood the importance of responding to Lynette's inquiries.

"An architect, huh? That means your good with your hands, right?"

"You could say so," Elijah smirked. His hand went to his chin and he bashfully rubbed his beard. "I pay attention to details, I guess."

"Have you designed anything I would recognize," Lynette asked.

"Possibly," Elijah answered.

"Like what," she smiled.

"Well, have you been to Lance and Samantha's home?"

Lynette's stilettoed feet stopped moving. When she turned in Elijah's direction her brow was slightly furrowed.

"Of course, I've been there," Lynette replied. "Sam is my best friend."

"Well, Ms. Jones, I designed their house," Elijah answered.

Lynette smiled because of the use of her government name. She'd been doing the same thing to him as a little jab. And then her eyes widened.

"Seriously?"

"Seriously," Elijah chuckled.

"That's not just a house, honey, that is palatial. It's a mansion! Their home is amazing, I mean it's more than amazing. It's a dream home!"

"Thank you, Lynette," Elijah replied. Hearing the accolades only made him flush more.

"Oh, we're on a first name basis now," Lynette teased.

"I would hope so, beautiful."

"Oh, now you're just flirting with me," Lynette said taking a step forward.

"Maybe," Elijah replied, falling in step slightly behind her.

"Mmhmm."

The two continued to walk through the chateau, appreciating the art, and engaging in easy conversation. When they arrived at a lit fireplace, Elijah asked if she wanted to sit down. She did, and the two took up residence on a wingback sofa immediately across from the crackling fire.

"So, tell me something about you," Elijah encouraged as they got comfortable on the couch.

"Well, I'm not sure what there is to tell," Lynette began.

"I want to know everything about you," Elijah encouraged.

"I work in the mailroom at Preston's, but I'm sure you already know that," she sighed.

"No, I didn't," Elijah replied. "As I said, the only thing I asked Lance was your name, nothing else."

"Does the fact that I work a menial job change the way you look at me, or whether you're still 'interested' in me?" Lynette emphasized the 'interested' with air quotes. She chuckled behind her statement, but the laughter didn't reach Lynette's eyes.

"Beloved, listen to me and hear me clearly. Please, don't ever diminish yourself with words. Words have power, you know? They have the power to make us feel a certain way about ourselves." Elijah paused for a moment before continuing.

"Nothing about you is menial. Your job doesn't define who you are. It's what you do, that's all. And there is a certain skillset, certain qualities that only you bring to that job." Elijah's voice seemed deeper, firmer, more resolute as he spoke. Elijah's eyes were intense, commanding that Lynette pay attention to what he was saying.

"True, we've only just met, but I consider myself a great judge of character. And you, Ms. Lynette Jones, are by no means menial."

Lynette lowered her eyes, avoiding his gaze. Elijah remained patient, giving her a chance to process what he was saying. Elijah meant every word and he didn't want her to miss a single one. Lynette's response spoke to something more than just her job. That's what Elijah spoke to. He reached out extending both of his hands, upturned for Lynette to accept. Looking down at his extended hands, Lynette sighed heavily before folding her hands into his. Elijah closed his hands around hers, gently rubbing them with his thumbs.

"And, let me say this," Elijah continued, tilting his head in an effort to regain her full attention.

"Your mind? Far from menial. Your heart? Your persona? Far from menial. And your suave, your genasaqua? Mmm," Elijah moaned, "not menial in the least."

Lynette eased her hand from his and fanned herself. Lynette's internal thermometer was rising, and Lynette knew no other way to quench the thirst she felt in her core; not now, not at the moment. She'd just met him.

"Is it hot in here all of a sudden," she giggled embarrassedly. She could feel color rising in her cheeks.

"We can change that," Elijah thrummed.

17

"How," Lynette asked flitting her long lashes.

"Come with me," Elijah suggested.

There was no hesitation on Lynette's part. She'd live an entire year mournfully celibate. It was more than just the absence of sex and Elijah's obvious sex appeal. There had been no meaningful connection with a man, no real prospect of a fulfilling relationship, no soul connection whatsoever. She missed that; the kind of energy that only a real man could provide.

4

The duo made their way to the lobby. Lynette admired the Christmas trees that lined the decorated entrance. Multicolor lights blinked on and off, casting rainbow shadows on the high polished marble floors. There was another roaring firing blazing in the floor to ceiling fireplace and Lynette found herself watching the flames dance. She could hardly believe what was happening. What were the chances of meeting a man like Elijah? Not what were the probabilities for a lucky person, but what were the chances for someone like her? It was unbelievable. At one point in Lynette's life, she prayed for God to send her the right man. It was a prayer she prayed religiously and consistently feeling like the choice shouldn't be left to her alone. But no one came, and truthfully, Lynette got discouraged. She stopped praying that prayer. Not that she lost faith in the Creator, but maybe, she was meant to be alone.

So, this, Elijah Sinclair, Lynette couldn't explain. She didn't even try. Whether it was fate, destiny, a fluke, a happy accident, Lynette wasn't sure, but she was willing to ride this one until the wheels fell off. If nothing came of it, Lynette would be okay with it. She liked that someone who seemed to be of substance was interested in her. Lynette enjoyed the ease of conversation and the way Elijah made her laugh. She appreciated how he looked at her; not with lust in his eyes but what seemed like general interest. Lynette was flattered and fascinated. Elijah made her feel desired and desirable. She was having fun, plain and simple.

"Ready," Elijah asked, sliding up beside her. Lynette startled, her shoulders jumping. She had been so lost in her own thoughts she didn't sense Elijah coming up beside her.

"Oh, I'm so sorry, beautiful," he apologized, seeing her alerted response. His hand instantly went to the center of Lynette's back, steadying her, grounding her. She relaxed into his hand. It was settling.

"Oh no, you're fine," Lynette replied, leaning into him. Elijah's body held firm as her body matched the length of him. "And I mean that both literally and figuratively," she purred.

"Ah, now who's flirting with who? Or is it whom?" Elijah hummed.

"Either way, I'm guilty as charged," Lynette confessed, laughing at her own bravado.

"I like it," Elijah whispered. "Come on," Elijah encouraged, once again reaching for Lynette's hand. She accepted; appreciating that he wanted to make physical contact with her. That said a lot; like he was not embarrassed to be seen with her, to touch her, to be affectionate towards her. That, in and of itself, was huge for Lynette, and different. She fell instep just behind Elijah.

"Where are we going," she asked, trotting up to catch up with his elongated stride.

"You'll see," Elijah offered with a wink and a brilliant smile.

They crossed the lobby. Elijah paused just before they reached the entrance. Lynette stopped and looked at Elijah wondering what the hesitation was about. His eyes trailed up and Lynette's followed. A smile eased across her lips as the mistletoe came into view, directly overhead.

"You wouldn't want to break with tradition, would you?"

Lynette smiled and then laughed. as her gaze lowered and found rest in Elijah's eyes, Lynette continued to smile.

"Who am I to rebel against tradition?"

The laughter faded from Lynette's lips as she watched Elijah slowly fold in his full lips and then release them slowly. Her eyes moved from side to side as Elijah gently lifted his hands and placed one on each side of her face. And when he leaned in, lovingly kissing Lynette on the forehead, her eyes closed, and she felt him, the energy of him, the soul of him move through her. The two stood in that moment. Elijah appreciated the softness of her skin against his lips. He inhaled her feminine essence, breathing in deeply. He noticed her exhale that matched his inhale.

When they reached the rotating front door, Elijah pulled Lynette in close, protectively holding her as they waited for the spinning glass door to open so they could step inside. Elijah checked in with her and the two took the step together. Elijah watched the entire time the door rotated. He wanted to ensure Lynette stepped out safely. Once they cleared the door, Elijah continued his protective hold on Lynette. She appreciated it as the air had a wintry crispness that caused an instant chill. Noticing her body shivering beside him, Elijah loosened the hold he had on Lynette and eased out of his tuxedo jacket.

"There you go," he said, placing the large jacket across her shoulders and adjusting it for maximum coverage.

"Thank you," Lynette replied, reaching up and pulling the jacket tighter around her.

"Always," Elijah replied.

It was the sound that first drew Lynette's attention. She thought she heard a bell ringing and then another sound she couldn't immediately distinguish. The noise drew her, and

Lynette turned in that direction. Her eyes brightened, and a smile moved across her lips. She looked up at Elijah.

"Did you do this?"

"Only if you like it," Elijah replied.

The smile remained plastered on Lynette's face as a majestic russet brown Clydesdale horse ambled up the drive. Behind him were a driver and carriage. When the driver called out and the horse stopped just a few feet in front of Lynette, her smile broadened. The horse was an incredible specimen.

"Come, beautiful," Elijah said, wrapping his arm around Lynette's waist and walking her to the carriage entrance. The driver had stepped down to be of assistance, but Elijah took care to make sure Lynette was successful in getting into the open-air carriage. Once Elijah was seated next to her, the driver regained his seat. Elijah reached across the carriage lifting a fur lined blanket and placing it across their legs.

"You must be cold," Lynette suggested. "Here, take your jacket."

"Sitting here next to you is keeping me warm enough," Elijah replied.

"Really now?"

"Without question," Elijah crooned. "Now, get on over here and help keep a brother warm."

Lynette giggled and did as Elijah suggested, scooting over on the seat. She pulled the cover over both their legs and then nestled in as Elijah draped his arm around her waist, pulling her in even closer. The carriage began to move; the horse walking in a slow rhythmic trot. As they snuggled close together, taking in the beauty of the landscape around them, and the beauty of the star-studded night sky, Elijah and Lynette continued to engage in casual conversation, getting to know each other a little better.

And when the conversation faded, and there was only silence between them, neither Lynette nor Elijah found it uncomfortable. Neither felt the need to fill the silence with empty meaningless words. They were both perfectly content simply being in each other's company.

Midway the ride the driver stopped the sleigh on the rest of a hill overlooking the vineyard below. The trail was lit with lamplights providing romantic ambient light.

"I have a thermos full of warm cocoa if you folks would like to have some. I make it especially for my passengers; a new batch each ride."

"That would be fantastic," Lynette replied.

The driver turned around, handing the warm thermostat to Elijah.

"Let me do that," Lynette said, reaching for the thermostat. The driver waited until they poured a cup of the steaming liquid before calling the sleigh back into motion. Lynette was careful not to overfill the cup. She blew on the edge of the warm liquid, cooling it, before offering the first sip to Elijah. She held the cup to his full lips and he covered her hands with his.

"Mmm," Elijah moaned as the warm, creamy liquid filled his mouth and warmed him internally as he swallowed.

He extended the cup to Lynette, helping her balance as she put it to her luscious lips.

Her moan was equally as evocative and music to Elijah's ears.

"That is good," she replied. "Here, there's a little more," she said, offering the cup to Elijah.

He graciously took the final sip, handing the cup back to Lynette which she screwed onto the thermos.

"You've got a little something there," she said, looking over in Elijah's direction.

"Where?"

Lynette pointed, "right there," she signaled.

When Elijah failed to figure out where she was pointing, Lynette lifted her thumb to his face and wiped the corner of his mouth. Before she could move her hand, Elijah reached up and gently guided her thumb to his lips. His eyes met hers as he kissed her there. The warmth of the cocoa couldn't compare to the warmth of Elijah's lips on her flesh. But the thermal sensation didn't stop with just Lynette's thumb. The heat of his impassioned kiss traveled the length of her arm to her chest and down her center. It was like a pulsing current Lynette couldn't contain. She could only imagine what kissing his lips with hers would be like. The wandering look in her eye drew Elijah's attention.

"Are you okay, sweet?"

"Yeah, I mean yes," Lynette, turning away from him. He caught her fantasizing, and Lynette didn't want Elijah to see her grimace. *Yikes!*

The rest of the carriage ride was just as magical. Lynette loved the way Elijah held her and he loved the way she felt in his arms; easy, natural, right. The driver delivered the duo back to the front of the chateau. And just as before, Elijah made sure that Lynette exited safely; lifting her by the waist and then turning and placing her gently on the ground. Lynette waited while Elijah tipped and thanked the driver. He escorted her back towards the hotel. Once they cleared the revolving door, Lynette stopped. Her eyes traveled upwards and Elijah's eyes followed. He smiled as he lowered his gaze, seeing the devilish yet slightly shy smile on Lynette's face.

"You wouldn't want to break with tradition, now, would you," she purred.

"Of course not," Elijah replied. Elijah's eyes held a sheen of purpose as he moved forward, eradicating any distance that previously existed between them. Lynette's entire being seemed to be filled with waiting as Elijah drew near to her. Slowly and seductively, his gaze drew downward, finding her amber eyes looking up into his. Lynette's heart lurched madly as Elijah swept her, effortlessly into his arms. The moment between Elijah coming closer and their lips finally connected was heightened with sexual, sensual tension. She nearly panted in anticipation as Elijah's lips found her; the first kiss whispering against her lips. His lips pressed against hers, then gently covered Lynette's mouth. She opened her mouth to his exploration. Lynette relaxed, sinking into the cushion of his embrace. And Lynette found herself opening herself to him, in non-physical ways.

Elijah's heart pounded ferociously in his chest as he felt Lynette relax into him. She tasted as good as she looked, and Elijah kissed her hungrily. When their lips parted, Elijah remained close. They breathed the same air.

"I have a new respect for tradition," Lynette smiled.

"I do, too."

"We better go," Lynette suggested, still speaking against the natural pout of Elijah's lips. She smiled as the soft hairs of his beard tickled her chin.

"I think we better," Elijah agreed.

The two walked hand in hand back towards the Paris ballroom; neither of them in a rush to return. They took their time, enjoying each other's company with each privately replaying the passion of the kiss they mutually shared. It wasn't until they stepped over the threshold of the ballroom did Lynette think about Samantha. *Oh my God. I forgot all about the reception*, Lyn thought to herself as her eyes tracked across the room in search of her best friend. Lynette didn't have to look far. Samantha spotted Lynette coming back into the ballroom and grabbing Lance by the hand, moved quickly in her direction. When Lynette looked up and saw the determined way Sam was moving, Lyn knew she was in trouble. She started thinking of an excuse, any excuse she could reasonably make for her prolonged absence. This time when Lynette's heart raced it was because she figured she disappointed her best friend.

"Where have you been," Samantha lovingly chastised; her

26

eyes moving between Lynette and Elijah. Lynette didn't know what to say.

"Hey bruh, what's good," Lance said, stepping up, giving Elijah a manly dap

Samantha stared at Lynette and watched as her friend blushed in front of her. Samantha didn't need for Lynette to say anything more. She walked over and threw her arms around Lyn's neck.

"I am sooo happy for you," Sam whispered.

"Don't get too excited," Lynette warned, even though she felt Sam's enthusiasm and shared some of it herself. Lynette thought it best to be cautiously optimistic.

"It's too late for that," Samantha beamed. "I can see it in his eyes."

The besties exchanged smiles. Lynette could only hope Sam's instinct was right. The two couples moved to the dance floor. The DJ had the place bumping playing a series of party jams including the Electric Slide that everyone got in on. The Moore girls and their significant others dotted the dance floor and fell in line when the Cupid Shuffle came on. There were plenty of smiles and lots of laughter to go around. And when the beat dropped, and the tempo slowed down, Elijah was right there, swooping Lynette into his arms and holding her close as their bodies moved in time to the music.

"Are you having a good time, beautiful?"

"The best time," Lynette replied.

They danced through the next three songs, holding each other close. He felt so good in her arms that Lynette couldn't think about anything else. She didn't want to. If this was a dream, Lynette had no desire to wake from it. When the tempo started to escalate again, Elijah held onto Lynette and guided her from the floor.

"Thirsty?"

"Yes," Lynette replied.

They walked together to the champagne fountain.

"Here, babe," Elijah said, lifting a glass for Lynette and then taking one for himself.

"Thank you, Mr. Sinclair," Lynette teased.

"We are so past government names now, don't you think," Elijah chortled; his eyes dancing and his lips parted on a smile.

"That we are."

"Do you have a New Year's wish," Elijah asked as they each sipped their champagne.

"Most people make New Year's resolutions," Lynette corrected.

True, but we are not most people," Elijah corrected.

"True, very true," Lynette smiled.

"Make a wish," he encouraged.

"I will if you will," Lynette replied coyly.

"I absolutely will."

Lynette closed her eyes dramatically and then peeked to make sure Elijah had his eyes closed. When she saw that he did, she closed her eyes in earnest and made her wish. *I want to be open to the possibilities...*

When Lynette opened her eyes, Elijah was still there, standing there waiting for her. They toasted their glasses, entwining their arms and drank to the wishes they made. Elijah drank Lynette in, still dazzled by her beauty and the refinement of her essence as he finished the champagne in his glass.

"I pray your every wish comes true," Elijah offered with an alluring smile.

"I wish the same for you," Lynette purred, feeling herself weaken under his allure and effortless charm. Their arms were still connected, and Lynette's glass was still near the curve of her mouth. Elijah leaned over and kissed the back of her hand. Lynette's already weakened stated nearly caused her knees to give way as she felt Elijah move through her; the whispered kiss to her flesh scathing a wave of intimacy that courted Lynette's heart. He lingered there feeling a blistering pang of desire that Elijah found hard to contain.

They watched the couples on the dance floor and enjoyed another glass of champagne.

As the last song faded, the announcer spoke.

"Has this been an incredible reception or what? Let's hear it for the lovely couple, Lance and Samantha!"

The crowd erupted into a boisterous roar. This isn't only a celebration of love, ladies and gentlemen. We are on the cusp of the promises only a new year can bring."

There was another round of applause and cheers from the crowd.

"It's almost that time, to ring in the New Year! Don't bring in the new year alone. Are you ready for the countdown?"

Just then, a woman approached the couple. She was still holding the bridal bouquet she caught earlier in the evening. Lynette watched her closely. The woman walked straight toward Elijah, never once making eye contact with Lynette. When the woman extended her upturned hand in Elijah's direction, Lynette's brow furrowed, but not faster than her feet moved. She put up a cautionary hand as she politely stepped in front of Elijah. Elijah smiled at the ease in which Lynette's freehand found the curve of her hip, accentuating the point she made. it was only then, the woman looked at Lynette. She had no choice as Lynette loomed large from her posture. The feigned smile the woman offered wasn't missed. With a shrug of the shoulders and a last look in Elijah's direction, the woman walked away.

Lynette pivoted on her heels, turning to face Elijah.

"Shall we," he suggested, extending a hand toward the dance floor.

"Absolutely," Lynette answered. Seeing the smooth smile on his lips was enough to straighten out the wrinkles in Lynette's forehead. Elijah led her to the dance floor and with one smooth motion, pulled Lynette into the solidity of him.

She felt the firmness of his chiseled chest as Elijah placed his hands on her waist.

"You're still frowning."

"She just don't know," Lynette fussed. "She coulda caught these hands." Lynette popped her lips and Elijah chuckled.

"For real," Lynette added, and then laughed at herself. Why she felt so protective of Elijah, Lynette hadn't yet decided. What she did know was that she couldn't imagine him dancing the last dance of the year with someone else.

"You had nothing to worry about," Elijah crooned reassuringly, easing his strong hands to the center of her back.

"Bet not have," Lynette smiled as she eased her arms around his neck. Elijah held her close enough that she felt his heart beating against her wanton flesh. Lynette rested her head against Elijah's chest and let him lead her, swaying in time to the rhythmic beat. She felt good in his arms. She felt right, Elijah thought to himself as his hands found the center of her back and he pulled Lynette in even closer. They continued to move in sync even as the music faded.

"Here we go!" The announcer said. "Let's count it down together. Ten," he began. And then on cue, the guests chimed in, "Nine, eight, seven..."

"I hope you know this is not the end for us," Elijah whispered in Lynette's ear as he held her in the curve of his muscular arms. Lynette felt the heat rising in her cheeks as her skin flushed warmly. "It's just the beginning."

And when the clock struck midnight, bringing in the new year, Elijah sealed his promise with a searing kiss.

❧ 6 ❧

"I hope you know, this is not the end for us."

That's what Elijah said to her. Lynette replayed that magical night over and over. She felt chills remembering the first time she heard the bass and timbre of his voice, melodically stroking her sensibilities. Her body tingled as Lynette recalled the first time she felt Elijah's strong but gentle hand at the center of her back. And when Elijah kissed her for the first time? Lynette swooned then, and she swooned now. The feeling was almost unexplainable. It was as if her heart melted from the overwhelming warmth that flooded her soul. Lynette laughed out loud when she remembered that woman; that wanton, flirtatious woman that approached Elijah. Lynette shut her down with the quickness, and she giggled thinking back on it. The two made a wish, each one private but completed in unison. And at the stroke of midnight, Elijah kissed her again. Lynette smiled, reliving the moments again as she prepared for her date with Elijah.

Elijah…

That kiss at midnight that caused a surge to move through Lynette like she never felt before; hot enough for a Princess Diary heel lift, remembering the way his scent filled her nostrils and the firm yet softness of his kiss. But Elijah didn't stop at just one kiss. They were still engaged in a heated, prolonged kiss long after the roar of the crowd died down and others abandoned the dance floor. The parting from the kiss was almost as salacious as the kiss itself. Their lips separated slowly as though neither of them wanted to separate. There was no drastic, stark separation. And afterwards, Elijah stayed there; close enough to kiss, his lips a mere whisper away. Lynette reminisced on how their breathing synchronized as they lingered in that special moment. Although there were hundreds of people around, Elijah and Lynette were the only two people in the room. They had a conjoined orbit; defying time and space together.

The smile remained on Lynette's lips as she ran her fingers through her curly tresses. Elijah and Lynette finally left the dance floor, hand in hand. For a moment, Lynette felt a nagging sense of sadness. The New Year had officially been rung in. There was no more cause for celebration and no reason for her night with Elijah Sinclair to continue despite what he said. It's not that she thought Elijah was dishonest in saying this wouldn't be the end. But handsome men said promising things to Lynette before. What they said was a lie. She hoped that Elijah spoke the truth. Everything about him said he did; unless Lynette read him wrong. She'd definitely done that a time or two. It was as though Elijah sensed a shift in Lynette's disposition.

"I'm starving," Elijah said as he pulled Lynette into him.

"I'm sure there are appetizers from earlier, and there's definitely cake," Lynette suggested.

"I don't want this fancy stuff," Elijah bemoaned. "I said I'm starving," he replied with an exaggerated sad face.

"Oh," Lynette smiled. "You want some stick to your ribs kind of food."

"That's what I am saying, beloved," Elijah smiled.

"The restaurants are probably closed in the chateau," Lynette mused.

"Who says we have to eat here," Elijah winked.

All Lynette heard was we. That meant their time together wasn't over.

"So, what do you suggest, Mr. Sinclair," Lynette purred.

Elijah leaned in, whispering in her ear. Lynette inhaled deeply; his sensual, masculine scent wafting into her nose.

"I suggest the two of us say our goodbyes to the happy couple and then get the hell out of here. What do you think? Because I want you to go with me. I'm not ready for this night to end."

Lynette absolutely melted; leaning in to the warmth of his breath against her ear. Elijah responded as Lynette hoped he would by kissing her sweetly there. The sweetness of Elijah's kiss resonated in Lynette's core. He wasn't like the other men who whispered nothings in her ear. Elijah whispered sweetly.

"You're leaving already," Samantha asked as Lynette and Elijah approached.

"I think they want to be alone," Lance suggested after eyeing the two of them.

"Uhn," Samantha smiled. "Well, in that case…"

The two friends shared a loving hug.

"He's one of the good guys," Sam shared with Lynette before their hug ended.

"I hope so," Lynette replied.

"I know so," Samantha smiled.

As Lynette separated from Sam, Elijah resumed his place by her side, wrapping his arm securely around her waist. Lance did the same with his new wife, and both women settled in to the reassurance they each felt.

"Well gone on then," Samantha said shooing the duo away. "Don't let us keep you."

As Elijah and Lynette started to walk away, Lynette looked over her shoulder and waved to Samantha. She was so happy for her best friend. Now, there was a chance Lynette could be happy, too.

The way he held her made Lynette feel light on her feet like she was floating on air. Elijah expertly navigated through the chateau until they reached the portico where his car was brought up. Lynette shouldn't have been surprised when the winter white, Bentley Mulsanne pulled up. Lynette was up to speed on the latest cars as a nod to her dad. He loved fine vehicles, and when Lynette dreamed about what a glamorous life looked like, she always included the car.

"Nice wheels," Lynette purred. She couldn't help herself.

"I'm glad you approve," Elijah smiled.

Elijah ensured that Lynette was comfortably in the passenger seat before rounding the back of the Bentley and climbing in on the driver's side. When Elijah fired up the ignition, Lynette momentarily closed her eyes, listening to the smooth hum of the engine. Elijah turned in Lynette's direction.

"Whatchu know about that," he chuckled.

"The sound of the engine," Lynette mused. "It's a powerful roar but quiet and understated."

"Oh," Elijah hummed. "So, the nice wheels comment was an understatement."

"It was kind of our thing," Lynette began, "between my dad and me."

Elijah could see Lynette's eyes light up and the easy smile that played on her lips as she continued. The love Lynette had for her father, Vincent was real and evident. One would think being the only girl would cause Lynette and her mother, Cynthia to be incredibly close. They had a good relationship. Lyn loved her mother, too. But she was a daddy's girl, through and through.

"Daddy didn't have a son to share his interests with, so he shared them with me. It was our bonding time. He loved cars from the classic to the futuristic. I guess it rubbed off."

"That's kind of sexy, Ms. Jones," Elijah crooned.

"I'm glad you think so," Lynette flushed.

The rest of their car ride was just as entertaining. They shared a bit about themselves with each other; not directly like question and answer, but more indirectly so that each revelation was an informative surprise. Lynette was so caught up in their conversation; she paid little attention to where they were going. When Elijah pulled his Bentley up to a 24-hour diner in the heart of the hood, Lynette was surprised again. She thought soul food, but she never expected the location. Once Elijah parked the car and exited, he came around to assist Lynette out. He walked closest to the street as they entered the diner. Elijah selected a booth and waited until Lynette was seated before removing his suit jacket and sitting across from her.

"Is that my boy?"

The boisterous voice from behind caused Lynette to turn around. A middle-aged man, slightly graying at the temples boasting a wide toothed smile moved in their direction. Elijah standing up and smiling drew Lynette's attention to him as the man walking their way greeted Elijah with a strong embrace.

"Uncle Bobby, good to see you," Elijah exclaimed as he returned the embrace.

"You are looking good young man," Uncle Bobby replied, taking a step back from Elijah and then hugging him again with an approving pat to the back. "I bet it has something to do with this beautiful lady sitting across from you," Bobby said as he turned his attention to Lynette.

"You noticed," Elijah replied, smiling in Lynette's direction.

"That tells me you've been gone too long, young man," Bobby laughed. "Nothing gets past me, especially a beautiful woman."

Lynette, this is my uncle, Robert Sinclair, owner, and proprietor of this establishment.

"Very nice to meet you, Mr. Sinclair," Lynette smiled, extending her hand to Elijah's uncle.

"That's Uncle Bobby to you, pretty lady and good to meet you, too," Bobby answered folding his thick hand gently over Lynette's.

"Now, you didn't come here for a family reunion," Uncle Bobby said to Elijah.

"That and I'm hungry," Elijah chuckled, regaining his seat.

"I'll get a menu for the lady," Uncle Bobby smiled.

"He eats the same thing every time he comes," Bobby said, leaning in Lynette's direction before padding to the front of the restaurant.

"Is that true," Lynette asked, intrigued by Elijah and his uncle's relationship.

"That I eat the same thing every time," Elijah repeated. Lynette nodded in reply.

"Absolutely," Elijah confirmed. "It's a craving that only my uncle's food can satisfy."

Bobby returned with the menu. "I'll give you a few minutes, Lynette to take a look."

"Thank you," she replied as she accepted the menu Bobby offered.

"I'm curious as to what you always eat here," Lynette mused as she perused the menu.

"Don't judge, okay," Elijah began.

"No judgment here," Lynette grinned.

"Okay, because not only am I trusting you with the best kept eatery secret in the A, but also my love of good food," Elijah contended.

"Your secrets are safe with me," Lynette replied smilingly.

Elijah rubbed his hand together as he continued.

"To start off, I have to have my uncle's honey bar-be-cue wings. Melt in your mouth delicious with a side of golden onion rings. Then, for the main course, Uncle Bobby's legendary shrimp and grits; more like prawns and grits, the shrimp are so large. And to top it off, whether I have room or not, I have to have a warmed slice of apple cobbler with pecans laced throughout, topped with homemade vanilla ice cream and a healthy drizzle of caramel for balance."

Elijah licked his sexy lips as though he could already taste the food. Lynette's eyes were immediately drawn to them, and she folded in her lips and slowly released them in response.

Lynette set the menu down. "Then I'll have what you're having," Lynette sang.

"Excellent," Elijah replied. "I hope you're hungry."

"That I am," Lynette answered.

Elijah signaled a waitress who conveyed their order to Uncle Bobby and then brought their drinks.

"I have a confession to make," Elijah said after taking a sip of his drink.

"And what is that," Lynette asked, taking a sip of her own.

"I had dual motivation for attending Samantha and Lance's reception," Elijah admitted.

"Dual motivation?"

"Yes, beloved," Elijah replied. "Of course, I was there to celebrate with the happy couple."

"And the second part of your motivation," Lynette queried.

"To see you."

"Me?"

"Yes," Elijah confirmed. "The reception was not the first time I saw you," Elijah continued. "I've seen you more than once, and I was hoping to see you again; approach you like I wish I had done before."

"Why didn't you," Lynette asked, finding it difficult to keep the flush that warmed her cheeks spilling over into a blushing smile.

"I was nervous," Elijah admitted. "I didn't want to be rejected."

Lynette extended an open hand across the table.

"What made you approach me tonight," she asked.

"Because," Elijah sighed, accepting her hand, "I wasn't willing to go into a new year with new possibilities and old curiosities without knowing, one way or the other."

"I'm glad you did," Lynette replied. Elijah folded his other hand over Lynette's completely covering hers.

"I'm glad I did too," Elijah answered with a penetrating gaze. "And I'm really glad you didn't reject me," Elijah chortled.

"I'm glad you were curious," Lynette guffawed.

"Me too, gorgeous."

"If you are anything like my nephew, you want your appetizer and your main course at about the same time. Tell me I'm right," Uncle Bobby bellowed as he approached.

"You are right," Lynette smiled.

They released hands as Uncle Bobby sat down the dishes of food. Steam rose from the dishes and Lynette couldn't resist inhaling deeply as her eyes drank in Uncle Bobby's culinary delights.

"This smells wonderful," Lynette replied as she sat back against the seat.

"And it tastes even better," Uncle Bobby beamed. "You two enjoy!"

Lynette and Elijah both placed their napkins in their laps as Bobby walked away.

"Will you say grace, Elijah?"

"Yes, I will."

They held hands once again and bowed their heads.

"Gracious father, we ask that you bless the food we are now about to receive for the nourishment of our bodies and bless the hands that prepared it. In your name, we pray, amen."

"Amen," Lynette chorused.

"Now, let's eat!" Elijah suggested.

Lynette hesitated, even though her palette was ready for what was to come. Elijah immediately noticed.

"What's the matter, babe? Not hungry?"

"No, that's not it," Lyn replied.

"Then what?"

"I want to eat," she started.

"Please, I want you to eat with me," Elijah reassured.

"I know," Lyn continued. "But, some men think women should be dainty when they eat, not eat too much, push the food away when they are still starving."

"I know men like that," Elijah replied. "However, I am not one of them. I love food, and I eat like I love food. I want you to do the same."

"No judgment?" Lynette asked.

"No judgment."

"Good, 'cause this food looks too good to eat delicately," Lynette laughed. She was glad to hear Elijah laugh with her. He put Lyn at ease, and it wasn't the first time she noticed. Lynette appreciated that. She also liked the fact that Elijah was willing to be comfortable with her. He wasn't standing on pretense although by societal estimations he had every right to be.

"And to make sure you don't fall into bad habits, I'm going to sit next to you, feed you if I have to," Elijah commented, lifting himself from the seat and repositioning himself next to Lynette. She reached over to adjust his plates, making sure they were easily accessible to Elijah.

"I don't want you to think when I am staring into the depthless eyes that I'm watching you eat," Elijah insisted, leaning over, laying his shoulder against Lyn's. The weight of Elijah pressed against her, made Lyn swoon a little; and it made her laugh. She liked that Elijah made her laugh.

"Don't let your food get cold," Elijah encouraged as he lifted a wing to his mouth. Lynette joined him, picking up one of the wings herself. She took her first bite.

"Mmm, oh my God," Lynette moaned. "This sauce is heavenly," she replied, taking a moment to lick the sauce from her index finger. "And the crisp on this chicken? Divine." It pleased Elijah that she liked the food. It pleased him more to see that Lynette didn't seem embarrassed to enjoy in his presence. Elijah chuckled when Lynette hummed again after tasting the shrimp and grits.

"Now you can't go telling everybody about my spot," Elijah reminded as they both leaned away from the table.

"I'm hijacking your spot, Elijah," Lynette answered, dabbing the corners of her mouth with the napkin. "Hope you don't mind."

Lynette turned fully to Elijah intentionally batting her long lashes and tilting her head slightly.

"Don't even," Elijah crooned, averting her desirous eyes and then being drawn back to look again. When Lynette recaptured his gaze, she slightly arched a single brow and then flitted her lashes again. "How am I supposed to resist that?" Eli asked; his voice throaty and low.

"You're not," Lynette simmered.

"Fine," Elijah conceded. "Our spot then," he hummed, leaning in and kissing Lynette lightly on the lips.

"I hope you two have left room for dessert," Uncle Bob said, moving towards the table.

"Uncle Bobby, I don't know," Lyn whimpered, patting her belly. That was until Bobby sat down the dessert. If the prior dishes were any indication, the smell, and the look was enough to make a person's mouth water, and the apple cobbler was no different.

"On no," Lynette moaned. "The smell? I don't know if I can resist."

"Don't," Bobby chimed. "Resistance is futile."

"It is," Elijah agreed. "Don't even bother."

"I'll pack up your leftovers and maybe even add a little

something extra to take home with you," Bobby said. "Eat up, beautiful lady."

"Elijah, I'm so full I think I'm gonna pop," Lynette sighed.

"Trust me, I understand. But, if you don't take at least one bite of my uncle's cobbler, he might be insulted." Elijah pulled a Lynette, slightly turning down his lips and hooding his brow.

"I wouldn't want to insult your uncle," Lynette acquiesced. "He seems like such a nice man."

"Then take just one bite," Elijah encouraged, taking a spoon of the warm cobbler, making sure to get a bit of ice cream and caramel drizzle. Elijah lifted the spoon to Lynette and watched intensely, as she took the sweet treat into her mouth. Lynette's eyes closed as she chewed slowly and then opened as she swallowed.

"Sinful," Lyn moaned. "That is sinful."

"Sin is good, sometimes," Elijah teased.

"It is," Lynette purred, lightly tracing her top lip with her tongue. "Just one more bite, please," Lynette smiled.

Elijah was more than happy to oblige.

A nd Elijah had been obliging ever since. After dinner,
Lynette and Elijah left with mounds of food, more
than their original leftovers. The ride home was just as enjoyable as their jaunt to the restaurant. Lynette trusted Elijah
enough to allow him to know where she lived; something she
would have never done under other first date circumstances.
Yet, when Elijah pulled into the driveway, neither of them
made a move to exit the car. It was as though the notion of
their time together coming to an end was something neither
wanted to accept. And so, they didn't. Their conversation
continued. Elijah and Lynette talked and laughed and talked
some more.

"I never even thought to ask you were you seeing anyone,"
Elijah observed.

"It would have been a wasted question," Lynette scoffed.

"Why do you say that," Elijah inquired, reaching over and
turning the radio down lower.

"I have been completely unlucky in the relationship
department," Lynette sighed.

"Why do you think that is," Elijah asked, genuinely
interested.

"You do not want to hear the sob story of my absent love life," Lynette posited, casually throwing her hand dismissively.

"Beautiful, I don't ask questions I don't want to know the answers to," Elijah replied. "With the exception of if you were seeing someone because if the answer had been yes, I don't know what I would have done."

"Yes, you do," Lynette rebuffed.

Elijah's brow raised.

"If what you said before is true, that you were interested in me before making your approach, you would have considered the possibility, and you, Mr. Sinclair, would have had a contingency plan in the event I was otherwise involved."

Contemplatively, Elijah stroked the sides of his face, weighing and measuring what Lynette said.

"You said that like you know me."

"I pay attention," Lynette replied.

"I see," Elijah smiled and nodded slowly. "You're right. I did have something in mind, just in case. I am glad it didn't come to that."

"Mmhmm," Lynette hummed, feeling satisfied with her deductive reasoning skills. Elijah seemed to be impressed.

"Back to your love life," Elijah not so passively suggested.

"It's sad, Elijah," Lynette replied.

"There's a reason though," he continued. "I'm just trying to get to know you better."

"I understand that," Lynette admitted, "But only if I get to ask the same of you."

"Definitely," Elijah acknowledged.

"You conceded that point a little too fast, Mr. Sinclair," Lynette taunted.

"Maybe," Elijah crooned. "You'll find out why soon enough."

There was a slight pause in their conversation as each sized up the other; their eyes individually trailing each other, searching for clues and insights they didn't already have.

Lynette sighed; her shoulders lifting and lowering before she replied.

"I am the kind of person who gives her all in a relationship; sometimes foolishly, when the other person wasn't or couldn't fully commit on the same level. I fell into the pattern of falling for potential, believing that if I supported that person, poured into them, lived their dream alongside them, then that potential would manifest into realized aspirations. It didn't turn out that way. Then I realized that after a while, I was trying to pour from a cup that was empty. I had given so much and got practically nothing in return."

Lynette searched Elijah's eyes for understanding. She found it there.

"I think I just resigned myself to the harsh reality that real love wasn't something I would have a chance to experience. And I was okay with that. I didn't really give myself a choice."

Elijah felt the pain Lynette tried to suppress. Although she told her story in a matter of fact tone, with little emotional inflection, Elijah sensed what she didn't say. Slowly, Elijah lifted his hand and lightly stroked Lyn's cheek. She leaned into his touch, and he lingered there as he started to speak.

"Our stories are not as different as you might think," Elijah began. "I too have had a less than satisfying experience in the relationship department."

Reaching up, Lynette took Elijah's hand into her own, resting their joined hands in her lap.

"That feeling of pouring from a cup that is empty, attaching yourself to someone who for whatever reason doesn't attach in the same way, it gets old and tiring. So, I understand the retreat. I understand shielding one's self from future hurt. I've done the same," Elijah admitted.

Lynette was surprised and slightly baffled by his admission. From everything she'd seen so far, Elijah was the dream man; handsome, a perfect gentleman, affluent, intelligent...

Elijah was a catch by many women's standards including Lynette.

"So, we're both doomed," Lynette sighed.

"No beautiful, I don't believe that. I refuse to believe that," Elijah insisted.

"Why?" Lynette questioned. "If we've both had such disastrous relationships in the past, isn't it wise, intelligent even, to just let it go and move on?"

"I can't live the rest of my life without real, passionate, mind blowing love," Elijah replied.

"I used to feel that way," Lynette sighed.

"I still do," Elijah rebuffed. "I believe that there is that one individual, designed solely for their perfect mate. I think the reason neither of us has found the kind of love we've desired before, is because our Creator designed soul mate had not yet manifested."

"That is so hopeful," Lynette whispered.

"You have to have hope," Elijah smiled.

By the time their conversation came to an end, the darkness of the midnight sky was giving way to a new dawn.

"I can't believe the sun is coming up," Lynette mused as she and Elijah strolled to her door.

"I can," Elijah mused. "You're so easy to talk to, to be around."

"And I can say the same, Mr. Sinclair," Lynette giggled.

When they arrived at the door, Lynette paused. There was a part of her that didn't want their time together to end. Elijah felt the same as his steps became more halty as they approached. Lynette reached in her clutch and pulled out her keys. Elijah held the screen door open as Lyn opened the main door.

"I guess this is good morning then," Lynette replied as she spun on her heels to face Elijah.

"The best morning, Ms. Jones," Elijah answered. Leaning forward Elijah closed the distance between them, kissing

Lynette passionately, causing her internal pressure to rise. It was a sweet kiss, not presumptuous but not innocent either. The kiss was just enough.

"Will you text me when you get home," Lynette asked, "to make sure you get home safe."

Elijah smiled warmly. "I can do that," he answered. "There's just one problem though."

"What's that?" Lyn asked.

"I don't have your number."

They both laughed. In all the time they'd spent together the notion of telephone numbers never came up. The two exchanged numbers and said good morning again.

I'll call as soon as I get home," Elijah promised giving Lyn a parting kiss on the cheek. Before entering her home, Lynette watched Elijah stroll down the walkway. She couldn't believe it. Elijah was amazing, and that walk? Lynette smiled as she closed the door. Elijah was true to his word to a certain degree. He did call, but Lynette could tell from the radio playing in the background that Elijah was still in the car. Lynette called Elijah on it, of course. And his response made her smile.

"I missed talking to you."

They did remain on the phone until Elijah made it safely home. However, the conversation didn't end there. It was like they had been apart for ages and just a few minutes ago because their conversation picked up right where they left off and enthusiastic as though they hadn't talked in forever. Lynette kicked off her shoes that she didn't realize hurt her feet until she did. The whole time she was with Elijah, Lynette paid her feet no mind. She even managed to undress and take off her makeup while she and Elijah talked. He told a few jokes that weren't funny. He has a dry sense of humor that is funny because it's so dry. Lynette laughed heartily at the jokes, bolstering Elijah to tell yet another one. Lynette couldn't remember a time when she had such a good time. She considered pinching herself just to make sure it was real. The sun was fully positioned in the sky by the time Elijah and Lynette ended the call. Lynette smiled as she did, thinking about Elijah's sexy ass walk from earlier.

And in just a few moments, Elijah would be strolling to her door and Lynette would melt again. She couldn't help checking the clock on her bedside table. She was anxious to see Elijah but in a good way. When the doorbell rang, a beautiful smile eased across Lynette's lips. Lifting herself from her makeup table, Lynette glided across the floor of her bedroom and headed down the hallway towards the front door. Lynette fluffed her hair one last time and folded her lips in releasing them slowly to ensure the gloss she wore was even. Lynette smiled as she opened the door.

"Good even, Mr. Sinclair," Lynette hummed.

"Good evening, Ms. Jones."

They both wore enchanted smiles, admiring each other.

"You look beautiful, as always," Elijah crooned.

Lynette flushed. She never got tired of hearing Elijah compliment her. It was different than the cat calls and pressured compliments she'd received in the past. Elijah looked handsome as well in dark denim jeans, that hung from his waist, grazing his muscular thighs before dropping down seamlessly to the top of his Italian loafers. The light blue button-down shirt Elijah wore graced his broad shoulders, tapering down against his taut waist. The dark gray jacket that echoed the line of Elijah's shirt polished off his casual dress look handsomely. Elijah couldn't keep his eyes from trailing over Lynette's sculptural frame. The nude blouse that Lynette wore low on her delicate shoulders was loose fitting; alluding to the swell of her breasts and the fine of her waist without giving it away. The tapered black jeans Lynette wore hugged the curves of her body in all the right places, and the black ankle boots with a golden wedge heel perfectly polished off her ensemble.

47

"Thank you, Elijah."

He assisted as Lynette closed her door and locked it. Lynette noticed a driver standing near the end of her driveway besides a white Cadillac SUV. Opening the back door, the driver assisted Ms. Jones in entering the vehicle and then waited until Mr. Sinclair was safely inside before closing the door.

"Another nice car," Lynette sighed as she ran her hand across the supple Italian leather seat. "Is this passive flirting," Lynette teased.

"I was hoping you'd be impressed, but, if I'm flirting with you, beautiful, you will know," Elijah smiled.

"A nice ride?" Lynette asked. "You're flirting," she cooed.

"Maybe a little," Elijah conceded. The two fell into easy conversation as the driver navigated through the Atlanta streets. Lynette's attention was drawn out of the passenger side window as they passed the historical Fox theatre, and the cable car passing nearby.

"The city has grown so much over the past decade or so," she began. "I'm glad that cultural sites like the Fox remain untouched."

"I see you have an appreciation for the nostalgic," Elijah mentioned as the car pulled to the curb. "I hope you'll enjoy our next adventure."

"I'm sure I will," Lynette mused.

"Thanks, Bishop," Elijah replied to the driver as the couple stood on the sidewalk.

"No problem, sir," Bishop replied.

Elijah took Lynette by the hand as the two meandered down the sidewalk. The early evening streets bustled with activity, but Elijah and Lynette were in no rush. They took in the sites as much as the people who moved around them.

"The Ferris wheel," Lyn sighed as they turned the corner. "Are we riding," she asked enthusiastically.

"Of course," Elijah replied.

Lynette's steps hastened as they moved toward the towering wheel, illuminated with bright neon lights standing stark against the evening sky. Elijah smiled as Lynette's eyes lit up, reflecting the bright lights before her. Lynette had seen the Ferris wheel several times, but she'd never taken a ride. This would be a first, and she was doing it with Elijah. That fact caused Lynette to smile even more. There was a short line of riders in front of Lynette and Elijah. Neither of them minded the wait. It was all about the time spent together. The wind rustled a little and Elijah was quick to wrap his arm around Lynette, shielding her from the breezy onslaught.

"Why here?" Lynette asked as she turned towards Elijah looking up into his handsome face.

"Because, even though our last date was a party, a wonderful celebration of love, the best parts of it were the times when it was just you and me, when it was quiet, just us," Elijah answered.

"Are you trying to steal my heart, Elijah," Lynette swooned.

"Without question," Elijah smiled.

That smile warmed Lynette's heart, and his words touched her soul. It didn't take long for the couple's turn to come around. Elijah helped Lynette into the ride's car and then entered himself. The ride assistant latched the door and Elijah wrapped his arms around Lynette's shoulders pulling her close. Lynette settled in against the strength of Elijah's strong chest. The ride started off slowly giving the couple a chance to take in the lay of the land in a way they hadn't seen it before. The ride was romantic and whimsical and classic. The view was amazing; but for both Elijah and Lynette, the magic was in their connection emotionally, physically, transcendentally. When the car they were in stopped at the top of the Ferris wheel, Lynette was a bit startled by the abrupt halt.

"You're not afraid of heights are you," Elijah asked feeling Lynette jump beside him.

"No, I wouldn't say afraid," Lynette began giggling behind her own surprise as she felt the car slightly rock underneath them. "Just had a flashback, that's all," Lynette explained.

"No, that's not all," Elijah laughed with her. "You have to tell me."

"It's embarrassing," Lynette fussed, pushing against Elijah's chest. When she looked into Elijah' eyes, he played sad and dejected which made Lynette laugh even harder.

"Eww, the puppy dog eyes," Lynette giggled. "You know I can't resist."

Elijah didn't change his expression even though he felt laughter bubbling up inside him.

"Fine," Lynette huffed. Shaking her head, Lynette went on. "The last time I was on an amusement ride, the car stopped much like this one. I was with a guy I was dating at the time, and we were with a group. Instead of him being concerned that the stalled car made me nervous, he started laughing and rocking the car hard to the point where I thought it was going to tilt over. I couldn't even blow it off I was so pissed and scared at the same time. His friends laughing and him joining in made it worse," Lynette admitted. "I've always loved rides like this, but it took me a minute to get over what happened."

Elijah wrapped his arm more tightly around Lynette.

"I know it sounds silly," Lynette confessed.

"Maybe," Elijah replied. Lynette shot him a look; one eyebrow raised and a slight tilt to her lips. "Let me finish," Elijah smiled.

"Go ahead, and you better make it good," Lynette teased.

"I was going to say that I am glad you didn't allow what some idiot did to you to ruin it for us."

"Me, too" Lynette smiled. There was a much stronger message behind Elijah's words that wasn't lost on either of them. Lynette was willing to put aside past hurts and take a chance; hopeful that the outcome would be better. Lynette was willing to take a risk. That spoke volumes for them both. When Elijah leaned in to kiss her, Lynette happily closed the distance between them. He was tender with her; yet Lynette felt the intensity of Elijah's lips enveloping hers, caressing hers. They were so engulfed in their heated exchange that neither paid attention to the slight jolt of the car moving again. The magnetism between the two was so intense; they didn't even hear the cat calls and cheers from those on the landing who saw them kissing. Their car came to a stop back where they started.

"I can send the car around again if you would like," the attendant suggested with a smile.

Lynette felt Elijah smile against her lips.

"JUST ONE MORE TIME," Elijah said, turning to the operator. This time the claps and cheers from the bystanders could not be denied as the attendant allowed the couple to remain on the ride. Elijah and Lynette picked up just where they left off as Lynette laced her arms around Elijah's neck and pulled him in for another tantalizing tango. This time it was Lynette smiling against Elijah's lips.

❦ 8 ❦

The Ferris Wheel ride was just the first stop of the night for Elijah and Lynette. In a lot of ways, the destination or activity really didn't matter. It was all about the duo spending time together. Although it was after shop hours, Elijah and Lynette strolled hand in hand in Buckhead window shopping, and then took a long leisurely ride to the Hartsfield Jackson airport to watch the planes take-off and land.

"If there was any place you could go in the world, beautiful, where would you go," Elijah asked tucking Lynette in the curve of his arm.

"And money was no object?" Lynette asked as she watched another plane ascend into the night sky. Even though Lyn had lived in Atlanta her entire life and been to some of the same places before, experiencing them with Elijah made it all feel brand new and exciting. And although Lynette was living the moments, she could hardly believe they were real. Like many other women who the patriarchal, sexist society considered past their prime for marriage, having children and having love in their life, Lynette had all but resigned herself to loving herself in the absence of someone loving her. She privately fantasized about what was, with no real thought to what could be. But Elijah...

He was encouraging Lynette to fantasize openly.

"Money is no object," Elijah encouraged.

"It's weird to think outside the confines of money," Lynette sighed. "This is definitely a fantasy," she laughed.

"Play along," Elijah smiled. "I am genuinely interested." Lynette stopped looking at the airplanes and turned her gaze to Elijah. His eyes and his lips smiled.

"Fine, Lyn replied. "Let me think, hmmm."

Elijah waited patiently, watching as Lynette put a delicate finger to her chin in contemplation.

"There are a lot of places I've thought about going," Lynette began. "Paris because of the romance, the Caribbean for the beautiful, turquoise water, even Africa, to touch the ground where civilization was born, the Mother Land," Lynette mused. "But I think the most unconventional place I've dreamed of going was to Alaska."

"Why Alaska," Elijah asked, intrigued by her reply. He wrapped his other arm around Lynette's waist and pulled her in even closer.

"The northern lights," Lynette replied.

"The northern lights?" Elijah could see Lynette's eyes dance as she continued.

"I know it probably sounds weird, but I think the idea of natural colors painted against the dark sky is magical. It's like God is showing off," Lynette smiled. "All those other places have natural wonders, but there is something about the Creator's midnight rainbow. I think it's fascinating."

Elijah couldn't resist smiling with Lynette. She made him excited, seeing the vision through her eyes.

"Okay, so I answered the question," Lynette said. "Now, it's your turn."

"How am I to follow such an incredible description,"

Elijah laughed. "All spiritual and things. I have no comeback for that."

"Right, Lynette scoffed. "It's probably because you've been everywhere."

"I have been a lot of places that's true," Elijah confessed.

"What was your favorite," Lynette asked laughingly pressing Elijah to play along.

"Canary Islands, Spain," Elijah finally answered.

"And what makes the Canary Islands so memorable," Lynette inquired as she cozied up to Elijah. For a moment, the feel of Lynette against his core made it hard for Elijah to focus. She felt so good pressed against his flesh that his mind began to wander to far more carnal places. When he fell, silent Lynette looked up, finding Elijah's eyes hooded and brooding. The fold and release of Elijah's bottom lip as his eyes roamed over her were enough to send a wave of pulsating heat to her core. His penetrating gaze made it difficult for Lynette to focus, too.

"The reason the Canary Islands are memorable is because of the black sand beaches; naturally black. It's so unexpected," Elijah whispered, enunciating every word with a kiss; first to Lynette's forehead then to the tip of her nose, and leveling the remainder of his sensual kisses to Lynette's lips. "Seeing your melinated skin against jet black sand, knowing the blackness was intentional, not accidental. It's like you said, one of the Creator's many wonders," he said with another mind-blowing kiss. "Just like you."

Lynette felt her heart pound hard in her chest as Elijah's words were like music to her ears. Lynette traced Elijah's handsome profile with her finger as her lips met his. She felt the urgency in Elijah's kiss as his lips captured hers, refusing to let go. Lynette didn't want him to either.

Once again, the sun was ascending when the couple returned to Lynette's home.

"Why is this part so difficult," Lynette sighed.

"If you feel like I do, you don't want our time together to come to an end," Elijah crooned.

"Exactly," Lynette sighed again.

"If I promise to see you sooner than later will that make it less difficult," Elijah asked, easing his thickly corded arms around Lynette's welcoming waist.

"Don't make promises you can't keep," Lynette taunted.

"You should know me better than that by now," Elijah corrected.

"I do," Lynette purred.

"Sooner, not later," Elijah repeated.

"Very soon," Lynette smiled.

They parted on a sweet yet steamy kiss, both finding it hard to leave the other. Elijah held on to Lynette as she pulled the key from her purse and opened the door.

"Text me, so I know you're safe," Lynette reminded.

"I will," Elijah agreed. He waited until Lynette was safely inside the door before pivoting on his heels and heading down the walkway. When Elijah didn't hear Lynette's front door close, he turned around again. A smile teetered on the corners of his lips when he saw Lynette still standing in the same position wearing a devilish grin.

"What are you doing," Elijah smiled.

"Watching you walk away," Lynette admitted. The sexy in Lynette's voice sent a surge through Elijah's core. He took a decisive step forward. It would be so easy to give in to his carnal desire. The same was true for Lynette. She could easily give in to the physical. But there was a part of Lynette that hesitated. She'd been down that road one too many times; thinking with her body, giving of herself too soon only to be woefully disappointed in him and herself. Although Lyn felt like Elijah was different, that he was somehow better than his predecessors, she wouldn't make the same mistake again. And if he was real and sincere, it would be worth the wait... she would be worth the wait.

"Uhn uhn, Mr. Sinclair," Lynette teased, raising a cautionary finger. "I need to see the full swagger."

She was sizing him up. Elijah was flattered and still tempted, but he complied, clearly more conscientious of his stride. He looked over his shoulder one last time. Lynette was still there watching. Even from where he was Elijah could see the smile on her face.

The next morning

THE PHONE RANG several times before Lynette picked up.

"I feel abandoned."

Lynette immediately recognized the voice on the other end of the line. She was still tired, and it felt like she had just gone to sleep.

"I would never do that," Lyn replied just above a whisper. Her voice hadn't quite woken up yet.

"It certainly feels that way," Samantha fussed. "I would ask why I haven't heard from you in the past few days, but I already know the answer to that," Sam continued. I got used to you dumping me every Monday night for that wretched WWE. But this new dumping? I feel some kind of way, Lyn."

"Mmhmm," Lyn moaned with a smile on her face.

"Lynette, I need all the details," Samantha playfully demanded, "so wake the hell up!"

"Come on, Sam. I just laid down," Lynette whined.

"It's ten o'clock in the morning, and you just went to bed?"

"Feels like it," Lyn admitted.

"Fine, go on and go back to sleep, but I need to see you today, no excuses."

"Uhnnn," Lyn moaned. She was desperately trying to hold on to the last vestiges of sleep.

"Seriously?" Samantha's tone was sharp and no longer as playful.

"Okay, okay, what time and where?"

"L'Arbre, two' o clock," Samantha insisted.

"Two o'clock," Lyn mumbled.

"For real, Lynette and don't be late."

"I won't, promise."

That last part was mumbled, and then the line went dead. "She better show up," Samantha laughed. She couldn't really be mad at her best friend; well, not for long anyway.

"What's up with your girl," Lance asked, rolling over and laying his head in Sam's lap. She felt the strength of his large hand hugging her thighs.

"She's been Elijah' d," Sam grunted.

"My boy," Lance laughed, griping Sam's thighs and nestling his head more comfortably in her lap.

"Whatever," Sam fussed. Her mouth formed an O as she felt the press of her man against her wanton flesh. No matter how many times he held Sam, caressed Sam, the feeling of enticement never got old.

"He's not going to steal Lyn from you," Lance offered. "She loves you, babe."

Lance lifted his head slightly, just enough to kiss Samantha's inner thigh. When he opened his mouth and suckled there, kissing and nibbling her there, Samantha moaned without restriction.

"But not as much as I do," Lance crooned. He bit her inner thigh again.

"Babe," Samantha whimpered.

Lance slid his hand between Sam's thighs and parted them. She willingly adjusted to his touch; her yoni crying out for sweet relief. Lance's carnal urges could not be controlled. With one moment, he lifted his tall frame between Sam's thighs and eased her panties to the side. She felt the lusty penetration of Lance's tongue; lovingly licking the folds of her jewel before easing his tongue inside her first; just a little at first but then more until his thick tongue stroked her G spot, hitting it over and over. Samantha's back arched under his pressing, and she slid down to meet his thrusts, opening her legs to him, opening her vessel to him completely.

When Samantha felt a much firmer touch accompanying the softness of Lance's tongue, Samantha winced and then moaned again. His finger stroke was deliberate and heightened the scintillating sensations between her thighs. Lance's manhood grew from the smell of her, from the taste of the woman he loved and craved incessantly. Her panties were in the way, and Lance refused to be denied. With both hands, he ripped the delicate covering from her.

"Lance…"

Just hearing Samantha call his name was enough to send Lace into overdrive. With one motion he lifted onto his knees, taking Samantha with him; her legs draped over his muscular shoulders. She felt the first wetness creaming from her jewel. Lance had the magic touch and Samantha was weak from it but not so weak that she couldn't guide his thickness into her welcoming womb. His swollen manhood felt good under Samantha's fingertips. She rolled her thumb across the head, making Lance's dick jump in her hands. She felt the first of his creaminess moisten her thumb. Lance's eyes followed her finger. He couldn't keep his animalistic instincts at bay. And the fact that he loved this woman more than life itself pushed him on. He had to have her. Samantha couldn't wait any longer to feel his fulness inside her. She guided him in, lifting her hips to receive him. But when she took that same thumb and raised it to her beautiful lips, licking and sucking his essence from her skin, Lance couldn't hold back. His thrust was deep and strong. He kept his eyes on Sam's mouth as he gripped her thighs pulling her into his downward stroke.

"Uhm, uhm, uhm," Lance groaned as beads of sweat appeared on his forehead.

He rocked her with every push, loving her as much as fucking her. Samantha's pert breasts rocked in rhythm with him. She panted against his push taking her arms and pressing her breasts together. When she lifted her hips higher, changing the angle of his fuck, Lance felt her puss contract around his dick, coaxing and caressing it like his manliness belonged only to her. He fucked Sam harder faster; the sound of her plump ass slapping against his thighs.

"Ohhhh, baby," Samantha cried out. "Fuck me," she panted.

He growled, low and deep. His thighs and ass muscles flexed as he lifted onto his toes, leveraging his weight inside her.

"Ah! Yes, baby, yes!" Samantha screamed.

Her folds moistened, releasing fresh dew onto his throbbing dick. Sam's eyes rolled to the back of her head as her body convulsed in climax. She couldn't hold on to it, not anymore. Lance was serving her, making Samantha breathless. She felt drops of sweat against her breasts as he pounded her.

"Babe, babe," Lance panted. "Damn girl!"

Her pussy was too good. Lance couldn't hold back as he felt a surge in his core. His hot sticky gism poured from it and filled Samantha to capacity. But his thrusts continued, and her hold on him didn't end there. Even after Lance collapsed into her lap, Sam's jewel held his dick, milking it for every last drop. They basked in the afterglow as Sam stroked his head while her puss throbbed against his flesh.

"Did you say something about loving me," Samantha smiled, running her fingers down the center of Lance's back.

"You already know," he moaned.

❧ 9 ❧

S amantha checked her watch. It was ten past two and Sam contemplated calling her friend just to make sure Lyn remembered they were supposed to meet.

"Where's your girl, Kennedy asked as she brought her big sister a drink.

"I have no idea," Samantha replied. "She was half sleeping when I spoke with her."

"I'm sure she's coming," Kennedy reassured.

"You're always so optimistic," Sam answered. "But in the meantime, how are you holding up?"

Samantha saw Kennedy rub her growing belly. When Kennedy dropped her eyes towards the floor, Sam's eyes naturally followed.

"Oh, poor baby," Sam answered. "Sit down, Ken, your ankles are huge."

"Girl, these are no longer ankles," Kennedy laughed. "Baby these are cankles!"

Sam loved hearing Kennedy laugh. Her laughter was soulful and so full of life. Ken did take Samantha up on taking a seat. Although she promised Bryce, her husband that she wouldn't overdo it, Kennedy had a hard time pulling back. L'Arbre was her baby, before the baby. She had her hands in everything from menu development to making sure every patron was pleased with their experience. Kennedy was constantly on her feet, and it showed.

"You are glowing though girl," Sam added."

"Thank you, girl, because I tell you, this baby is wearing me out," Ken giggled.

"Well, I can't wait to meet my little niece or nephew," Sam smiled.

"Sorry I'm late," Lynette offered, sauntering up to the table.

Lynette was intimately familiar with L'Arbre. She'd been there several times with Sam and several of the Moore sisters.

"Hey girl," Kennedy smiled. Lynette ambled over to the owner and gave her a big hug. She made her way around the table and hugged Samantha as well.

"I guess I forgive you," Sam smiled.

"Charge it to my head and not my heart," Lyn replied as she took the seat across from Samantha.

"I'll let you girls get to it," Ken said, slowly getting to her feet. "I'll send the waitress right over."

"Ken, are you sure? Resting a few more minutes couldn't hurt," Sam suggested.

"Girl, I'll be fine," Kennedy insisted. "I hope." Ken smiled as she walked away.

"I wasn't sure you were going to make it," Samantha said, turning her attention to Lynette.

"Girl, I almost didn't," Lyn admitted. "It was so hard getting up."

"Elijah?" Samantha smiled.

"Girl, even in my dreams," Lynette laughed.

"He's all up in your dreams?" Sam smiled.

"Yes," Lyn guffawed. "Even after a wonderful date that

lasted for hours, that man still managed to creep into my dreams. Whew!"

"Oh, so is that why you was all moaning and groaning on the phone?"

"I did not," Lyn protested.

"Oh, but you did!" Samantha clapped back. "So, it's going well," Samantha asked, taking a sip of the white wine spritzer Kennedy provided.

Lynette's laughter faded far too quickly. When Lyn sighed, Samantha looked up over her glass.

"Really, Lyn?" Samantha asked and sat her glass down.

"I can't help it, Sam," Lynette confessed.

"Talk to me," Sam encouraged. She knew that sigh all too well. It wasn't a sigh that said everything is going great and I am so happy. It was the sigh that said, I don't trust what's happening right now. Samantha knew it well because she'd sighed the same way in the past. Conversation ceased for a moment as the waitress approached with menus.

"Something to drink, ma'am," the waitress asked.

"I'll have what she's having," Lynette replied.

"Is it okay with you Lyn if we order the house special," Samantha asked.

"Sure," Lyn answered. "Everything at your sister's place is amazing."

"Two house specials then?" The waitress inquired.

"Yes. that will do it," Samantha answered. The ladies handed back the menus and waited until they were alone again.

Okay, Lynette, tell me what's going on," Samantha said.

"Can't we talk about the honeymoon instead? How much I missed you? Anything else?"

"We can," Samantha replied. "Honeymoon was amazing. You didn't miss me that much because you didn't call," Sam huffed. "And anything else? Right after you tell me what's going on with you."

"I don't want to sound like a broken record," Lyn huffed. "Getting all excited prematurely only to have my hopes dashed against killer rocks."

"That would be fine if you hadn't endured all my broken record conversations," Sam insisted. "I'm your friend, Lynette. It's my job to listen. Besides, who else are you going to talk to about this?"

The sigh this time was heavier, but Samantha was right.

"There is so much about Elijah that is so right," Lynette began. "So much. And I want to trust my gut and my sixth sense, and my perception and everything else that's supposed to guide you in decision making. But I think my gut is broken," Lynette woefully admitted.

Samantha smiled, and it threw Lynette off.

"What's that smile all about? My gut is broken, Sam. I don't see nothin' to smile about."

"I'm smiling because we are so much alike, Lyn," Samantha clarified hoping Lynette would understand. "A broken gut? You know I know, hell. What's past broken cause that's what mine was, and you were the one who talked me through it. Remember?"

"I remember," Lynette admitted. "But talking about it and feeling it are completely different."

"I understand that," Sam answered. "So, tell me this has Elijah given you a reason not to trust what's happening between the two of you?"

"No," Lynette confessed. "But that doesn't mean anything. He could really be good at it, playing the long game."

"Okay, has he tried to pressure you past your comfort zone rushing you into saying or doing something you're not ready for?"

"No, Elijah has been incredibly patient," Lyn agreed. "I think I'm the one struggling with that."

"Oh, you want to jump his bones, huh?" Samantha taunted.

"Girl," Lynette gasped leaning in. "He is just mmm, irresistible."

"I hear you," Samantha giggled. "But you've managed to hold it together?"

"Barely," Lynn laughed.

"What are you two going on about," Kennedy asked as she approached the table placing the girls' orders on the table.

"Chile, relationship stuff," Samantha answered, and then inhaled deeply as she took in the enticing smells presented before them.

"Lobster mac and cheese, my famous Cole slaw, and some delicious garlic bread. The lobster tails are on me," Ken added.

"You are too kind, Kennedy, thank you," Lynette offered, taking her napkin from the table and folding it across her lap.

"No problem," Ken answered. "Make sure you leave room for dessert though, Ken encouraged.

"What do you have today," Samantha asked, knowing that desserts were an L'Arbre specialty.

"Well, we have bananas foster, red velvet cheesecake brownies, and Louisiana pecan pralines," Kennedy announced.

"Whew chile, I just gained five pounds hearing that," Lyn laughed.

"And when you taste my sweet treats, it'll be more like ten pounds," Ken laughed.

"Come on and sit down with us, Ken, Samantha encouraged. "I can use your help."

"What? For a Moore girls double-team," Lynette countered.

"If that's what it takes," Samantha rebuffed. She didn't even respond to Lyn's raised eyebrow and wrinkled nose.

Kennedy pulled out her chair and took a load off. Immediately a waitress appeared to see if there was anything the boss needed.

"Some cucumber water with a lot of ice and a spoon," Kennedy replied.

"What's that all about," Sam inquired.

"Honey, this baby is so fickle," Ken laughed. "I still haven't figured out what he or she will tolerate as far as food is concerned. But cucumber water and ice are a go!"

The ladies chorused in laughter.

"But enough about me," Kennedy said, rubbing her growing baby. "What's this relationship stuff you ladies are discussing?"

"Care to share, Lynette," Samantha asked. Lyn rolled her eyes as Kennedy turned her full attention to her.

"Due tell, Lyn," Kennedy encouraged. "I hope it's the guy from your reception Sam."

"It is," Samantha agreed.

"So, what's the matter girl?" Ken asked. "That man is fine!"

"He is," Lynette agreed. "And how does Bryce feel about your masculine observations?"

"Honey, I am happily married, but I for damn sure ain't blind," Kennedy laughed.

"I know that's right, sis," Samantha chimed. The sisters shared a high five.

"Ya'll are a mess," Lyn laughed.

"True," Kennedy replied. "So, what's the matter with you and the handsome guy?"

"Elijah," Lynette added smilingly.

"Mr. Elijah Sinclair, girl," Samantha added, "incredible architect, a multimillionaire, fine as hell as we all agree, and perfect for my best friend."

"He does sound yummy," Kennedy smiled. "What am I missing though?"

"Lynette?" Sam prodded.

"I don't trust my gut," Lynnette confessed, resting her hands in her lap.

"Her gut is broken, so she doesn't believe what's going on with her and Elijah is real," Samantha went on.

"Whew, chile, I think we can all relate to that," Kennedy added. "Of course, I don't know you as well as Sam, and I don't presume to speak for your situation. But let me say this. It's a lot of folks, women, and men, who struggle with trusting what we feel, especially when we've been hurt in the past."

Kennedy paused as the waitress returned with her water and spoon. After thanking the waitress, Kennedy promptly reached over to Sam's plate and scooped a small spoon of lobster macaroni.

"Taste testing," Ken smiled.

"Mmhmm," Samantha moaned, playfully slapping at her sister's hand.

"It is good though," Ken smiled after her tasting.

"That's for damn sure. So, don't reach over here again," Samantha quipped.

"Anyway," Ken pressed, "What would it take for you to believe that you can trust what you feel, Lynette?"

"I have no idea," Lynette replied. "I've been playing defense so long."

"Protecting your heart?" Samantha asked.

"Definitely," Lyn admitted. "It is no fun being made a fool of."

"Girl, been there done that," Kennedy agreed.

"That's for damn sure," Sam co-signed.

"Everybody plays the fool, sometimes," Ken sang.

"No exceptions to the rules," the three ladies sang and rocked in unison.

"Listen, baby!" Ken bellowed. They all howled with laughter, especially when other people in the restaurant started to rock and sing with them.

"Here's the thing, Lynette," Sam began. "You can only be made a fool of if you open yourself to the possibilities."

"Or," Sam added. "If you close yourself off from trying."

"Good point, sis," Ken chimed.

"I'm telling you, when I was going through my stuff, Lyn was the one who helped me to rise above my emotions so I could think clearly. It wasn't easy, but it was necessary."

"That's the thing," Lynette started. "I'm not sure what I feel is real; based on real things or whether Elijah is just an illusion. It's so frustrating."

"I get that," Kennedy sighed. "It sounds to me like Elijah has little to nothing to do with this."

Lynette's brow wrinkled. She looked across the table, seeing Samantha nod her agreement and then returned her gaze to Kennedy.

"What you're saying has nothing to do with him," Kennedy replied. "Regardless of what he says or does or doesn't say or doesn't do, matters far less than whether you are truly open to what he says does, doesn't say or doesn't do. Make sense?"

"I think so," Lyn answered.

Ken and Sam could hear the hesitancy in her response.

"It's all about you Lyn." Samantha began. "If you don't give yourself permission to feel what you feel based on the present, not the past, it won't matter what Elijah does. You are holding yourself back not because of Elijah, but the assholes who came before him."

Samantha's statement hit home. Lynette had been apprehensive about acknowledging her feelings even though they felt real to her.

"Let's keep it simple," Kennedy suggested. "Lyn do you like him?"

"Yes," she readily admitted.

"Is he nice to you?"

"Always," Lyn confessed.

"Has he done anything to remotely suggest that he is a wolf in sheep's clothing?

"Never, not once."

"And how does the fact that Lance and I both vouch for him; that I would never do that if I thought he wasn't worthy of you, and that I will kill a nigga about you weigh into your feelings?" Samantha clarified with a soul sisterly neck roll and an 'I don't play that shit' turn on her lips.

"That should make all the difference in the world" Kennedy added. "You can trust your friend when you can't trust your gut. You know Sam looks out for you like you look out for her."

"That's true," Lyn confessed. "I hadn't thought about that part."

"I know!" Samantha fussed. "Too busy rambling around in your own head, but I get it, for real."

"That girl that seemed so happy at the reception, where is she?" Kennedy asked.

The smile that slowly infiltrated Lyn's lips was undeniable. She remembered the first time Elijah approached her, the gentlemanly way he dealt with her, the first kiss under the mistletoe. She breathed deeply, blowing the air out slowly between slightly parted lips.

"She's right here," Lyn sighed.

"Good," Ken replied. "Cause that man is a catch, honey. Don't let him get away."

"Exactly," Sam agreed. "And Elijah already knows. If he does anything and I do mean anything to hurt you, he has to answer to me. And he don't want none of this. Trust!"

"Thanks, Ken. Thanks, Sam."

"Anytime girl," Ken chimed. "You're gonna have to start coming to brunch. "It's like relationship therapy."

"Straight up," Sam giggled. "Girl, they didn't let me get away with anything when I was speculating about Lance."

"Same thing here," Ken admitted. "Nailed my ass about Bryce."

"But it was all in sisterly love," Sam added.

"We have to be here for each other, girl," Ken continued.

"True," Samantha agreed. "But right now, I need to be here for this macaroni!"

10

The girls spent the better part of the afternoon eating, laughing, and sharing. Kennedy made sure neither Samantha or Lynette left the restaurant empty handed. She packed up a second helping of their entrees as well as each one of the desserts for them to enjoy later. When Lynette finally got to her car, she leaned back, resting on the seat. Her belly was full, and she felt relieved, somehow. The conversation had been stimulating and gave Lynette plenty to consider. But hearing from women she trusted, who she knew had her best interest at heart also gave Lynette permission to accept the way she felt about Elijah without second guessing its authenticity. It didn't mean that Lynette didn't have to proceed with caution. The Moore sisters didn't suggest she act foolishly or blindly. They suggested that she give Elijah a real chance to be the man Lynette already thought he was.

Lynette's phone buzzed. Reaching in her purse, Lyn pulled the phone out, and she smiled. It was like Elijah had ESP or something.

"Are you watching me," Lyn hummed.

"Why do you say that," Elijah chortled. He was just

leaving a client's home showing new drafts for their bed and breakfast.

"Because, I was just thinking about you," Lyn confessed.

"Interesting," Elijah replied. "I called you because I was thinking about you too."

"Really?"

"Absolutely, Elijah admitted. "It seems like here of late all I do is think about you."

"Aw, Elijah, that's so sweet," Lynette sighed.

"And true," Elijah continued. "That's why I need to see you."

Lyn felt a fluttering in her stomach. All she could do was shake her head and smile. That feeling felt real.

"I would love to see you, too, Elijah."

"I'm so glad you said that," Elijah lit up. "Tonight, eight o'clock. I'll pick you up, okay beautiful?"

"How can I say no?" Lyn flushed. "Goodbye, Elijah."

"Hold on a sec, beautiful," Elijah began. "Never said goodbye. Say see you later or talk to you soon but with me, never, never say goodbye," Elijah insisted. "Goodbye is final and too permanent, and I don't want final with you. I want to always know that you will talk to me soon or see me later. Understand?"

Lynette had never considered a closing salutation in that way. But what Elijah said made perfect sense.

"I understand, Elijah," Lynette replied. "I can't wait to see you later."

"I can't wait to see you later," Elijah seconded.

There was a long quiet pause before the line was disconnected, neither wanting to be the first to hang up. Lynette held the phone close to her chest and exhaled.

"Too much I tell you," she said aloud. "Elijah Sinclair? You are just too much."

Lynette couldn't languish in the parking lot although her dreamy thoughts were already with Elijah. Reaching in her purse and retrieving her keys, Lynette started the ignition. She had to get ready. She had to get ready for Elijah. Putting the car into gear, Lynette reached over and turned up the radio.

"Hey," Lynette sang as the smooth sounds of Make it Last Forever by Keith Sweat came through her surround sound. She danced in her seat as she moved the car out into oncoming traffic. Her mood was too good for even Atlanta traffic to spoil.

LYNETTE STOOD in her closet trying to figure out what to wear. She'd been so eager to see Elijah she didn't think to ask where they were going.

A devilish grin parted Lynette's full lips. She stepped out of the closet long enough to retrieve her cell phone. She found Elijah's number and sent a text.

Whatever shall I wear?

Lyn couldn't stop smiling. It was something about Elijah that kept her smiling. She padded back to the closet and stood there, looking at her clothes and waiting for his reply. It didn't take long for Elijah to answer.

Wear something warm.

Lyn laughed out loud. He slid a wining emoji behind his

comment. With any other guy, he would have lost major cool points for something like that. Lynette would have thought it corny. But with Elijah, the emoji only made Lynette smile. Now she could look in her closet in earnest and find something appropriate to wear; something warm.

Elijah built up an expectation of timeliness, and he didn't disappoint. At Eight o'clock Lynette's doorbell rang. Lynette didn't even bother stopping at the hallway mirror. She folded her lips in, evening out her lip gloss and opened the door. Seeing Elijah's handsomeness on the other side of the door never got old either.

"Elijah," Lynette sighed.

"Beautiful," he answered.

There was a mutual trek over the length of the other; Lynette taking in Elijah's light denim jeans, red turtleneck and midnight blue pinstripe jacket, thinly piped in red. And Elijah's eyes lingered as he enjoyed the elegance of Lynette's neck lightly covered by a high neck gray sweater that billowed slightly over black curve hugging jeans tucked inside knee-high black boots.

"You take my breath away," Elijah strummed, reaching out his upturned hand which Lynette graciously received. Elijah stepped forward closing the door behind her and accepted Lyn's door key as she handed it to him, locking the door securely behind her.

"Are you ready?"

"Yes, Elijah, I am."

As they traipsed hand in hand down the sidewalk, Lyn's eyes naturally traveled to the driveway. She wasn't surprised by seeing the chauffer. She was much more interested in seeing what car Elijah was picking her up in. Lynette stopped cold in her tracks.

"No way," she uttered as her eyes widened taking in the 1950 candy apple red four door Chevy Deluxe Hot Rod

Coupe. It was an old school classic car, and Lynette couldn't keep her mouth from falling open as they got closer.

"No way," Lyn sighed again.

She ran her hand across the curved bumper and the high polished chrome handle of the door.

"Get in," Lynette said turning to face Elijah. "I can't wait to hear how she sounds."

"How do you know it's a she," Elijah asked as the driver opened the rear door for them to enter.

"Because, anything this beautiful must be a she", Lynette purred.

"Touché," Elijah agreed.

Once they were securely inside, the chauffer closed the door and then walked around the back of the vehicle before climbing in the driver's side. Lynette awaited anxiously for the driver to turn the ignition. When he did, Lynette closed her eyes listening to the melodic rumbling of the engine.

"Nice," Lyn sighed. "She's nice."

"Her name is Candy," Elijah answered.

"Well Candy sounds amazing."

"Maybe you'd like to drive her?"

"You already know I would," Lynette beamed. "But for now, I am happy just riding."

Elijah smiled as he wrapped his arm around her shoulders. Lynette settled into the curve of the seat as the classic car moved underneath them. She loved everything about the car from the small triangular side windows to the detailed dashboard that screamed the 1950's. She was almost disappointed when their ride ended. But that disappointment didn't last long as Lyn looked out of the window seeing the private jet that sat at the end of the tarmac.

"Elijah," Lyn sighed.

The Chevy came to a stop, and the driver exited, opening the back-passenger door for them to exit. Elijah stepped out first and then helped Lynette to her feet. He held her hand as they moved down the red carpet that led to the plane.

"Good evening, sir, ma'am," a stewardess on the tarmac greeted them.

"Good evening Bianca," Elijah replied. "This is Ms. Jones."

"Good evening, Ms. Jones," Bianca greeted. Lynette nodded her head in reply.

"The captain advised that we will be ready for departure in about fifteen minutes.

"Excellent, Bianca, thank you."

Elijah mounted the steps that led to the interior of the plane, ensuring that he held Lynette's hand securely as she graced the stairs. Once inside, Lynette looked around at the luxurious surroundings.

"We go from nice to really nice," Lynette replied, taking in the Italian leather chairs with foot rests, mahogany interior and comfy couch.

"I'm glad you like it," Elijah answered. "Shall we get seated?"

"Yes, Lyn answered, feeling Elijah's strong hands gently grabbing her waist as he ushered her forward. Instead of stopping at the captain's chairs, Elijah led Lynette to the couch.

"We can sit here when the plane takes off?"

"In my plane, we can," Elijah replied.

Well then," Lynette guffawed, taking a seat. Elijah took up residence next to her, reaching over and buckling Lynette's seatbelt. Almost on cue, Bianca appeared, rolling a cart in front of her. Bianca handed a glass to each of them and filled the glasses with Dom Perignon. When she was done, Bianca sat the champagne in an ice bucket.

"Anything else before we take off, sir?"

Elijah looked to Lynette before replying. When she shook her head no, Elijah returned his attention to the stewardess.

"That will be all, thanks, Bianca."

As Bianca made her exit, Elijah turned his attention to Lynette.

"I would like to make a toast," Elijah proposed.

"To what?" Lynette asked.

"To you, beloved, for being the incredible woman I hoped you be when I watched you from afar."

"You are about that heart stealing thing again, aren't you," Lynette asked as they clinked their glasses together.

"Every chance I get until I have it, and you," Elijah strummed.

"Are you sure about this," Lynette asked fluttering her thick, mink lashes.

"I've never been surer of anything in my life," Elijah insisted.

I don't know what to say," Lynette mused.

"You don't have to say anything Lynette," Elijah crooned. "Just kiss me."

"With pleasure," Lyn purred.

Their entanglement was as heated as it had ever been. The rev of the jet's engine did nothing to stall their passion-filled exchange. Even after the jet ascended past the clouds, Elijah's lips caressed Lynette's in a way that made her heart soar. As their lips parted, they lifted their glasses again, quenching their tastes with the fine libation.

"Don't you want to know where we're going," Elijah asked as they settled in, sharing chocolate covered strawberries with whipped cream and even more champagne.

"It doesn't even matter," Lynette replied. "As long as I'm with you, handsome, where we go doesn't even matter."

"Still, I hope you'll be excited about our destination," Elijah chortled.

"I'm sure I will," Lynette answered.

11

The ride was as enjoyable as any time the two spent together.

"Good evening, the captain's voice emerged over the intercom. We should be starting our descent in just a few minutes. The weather in Anchorage, Alaska is a clear twenty-five degrees. Please buckle your seatbelts as we descend."

Lynette spun around on the couch. "Did he say Alaska? As in northern lights, Alaska?"

"Yes, he did," Elijah smiled.

Lynette gushed throwing her arms around Elijah's neck and squeezing him tightly.

"You are too good to me, Elijah," she smiled, leveling a sweet kiss to his cheek, one then the other.

"And I will always be if you let me," Elijah whispered against her ear.

Lynette's release was slow. Her eyes found Elijah's and she held his intense gaze.

"Elijah, what do you mean?"

Lynette had to ask, the pounding of her heart and the shiver down her spine said she had to ask. This was not the time to be presumptuous or to read more into what she thought she heard than she did. Lyn needed to understand precisely what Elijah meant, no speculation.

"If you give me the chance, I will love you, I will take care of you, and I will always be good to you."

There was not one moment's hesitation in Elijah's response nor any wavering in his voice. His eyes never left her, rendering Lynette nearly speechless. Elijah's eyes narrowed, and his brow furrowed slightly. His gaze was so intense, Lynette felt as though Elijah saw right through her.

"Lynette Jones, I have loved you since the first time I laid my eyes on you. I didn't know it was love at the moment. What I did know is that I couldn't sleep, I couldn't think of anything or anyone but you. And when I did finally sleep even my nighttime thoughts were always of you."

The words poured from Elijah's spirit as much as they came from his mouth. He couldn't stop them even if he tried. Elijah's heart was so full.

"I know now that the churning in my stomach, the unrest in my spirit, the ache I feel every time I leave your presence can't be anything but love; as unsettling and as frightening and as exciting as it is. Lyn, I love you. I can say that without reservation. And that doesn't mean you have to love me back. I have no right to expect that of you. But I wanted you to know. I'm sure my timing sucks, and it may be premature but-
"

"Shh," Lynette insisted. "Stop talking, Elijah," she said, placing a delicate finger against his lips.

Lynette's eyes misted over as her heart leapt in her chest. Her cup runneth over from hearing what Elijah said. She smiled looking at Elijah with his brow raised and speculation in his eyes.

"You had me at I love you," Lynette exhaled. She lifted her hand and stroked the back of Elijah's neck, never dropping her eyes from his.

"Your timing is perfect because," Lynette paused, fighting

back the tears. "I love you, too, as crazy and insane as that sounds. Elijah Sinclair, I love you."

The first tear fell to Lynette's cheek, but before it could move any further, Elijah kissed it away. There was this pull, this magnetism that neither of them could contain or deny. They held each other as the jet descended. No further words needed to be shared.

When the jet settled on the runway, Elijah unbuckled their seatbelts and helped Lynette to her feet. Her attention was drawn to Bianca as she made her way down the aisle.

"The equipment you requested, sir," Bianca said, extending parkas, hats, scarves, and gloves to the duo.

"You've thought of everything" Lynette sang, turning in Elijah's direction. She pivoted on her heels. "Thank you, Bianca."

"Absolutely, ma'am."

"Let me help you with your jacket," Elijah suggested leaning in and whispering against Lynette's ear. The warmth of his breath caused a heated surge to her core. The press of his body against hers sent another shiver much lower to her erogenous zone. Lynette acquiesced extending her arms as Elijah slid on the matte chrome parka. She liked the fact that Elijah's jacket matched hers. When he was done, Lynette made the same suggestion, helping Elijah get into his. Once their gloves and scarves were on, they exited the plane. Lynette could immediately tell the difference between Georgia and Alaska as the cold breeze blew against her exposed skin. Quickly Elijah huddled her up and escorted Lynette to the awaiting vehicle; an RV decked out with the latest gadgetry to make it as much like a moving house as possible.

"Can I drive this, too," Lynette asked excitedly.

"Anytime you want," Elijah answered.

"Good answer," Lyn smiled.

It was a short jaunt to the optimal location in which to view the northern lights. Elijah sat next to Lynette as she gazed out of the window; seeing the high snow drifts covering every surface; something she'd never seen before. Georgia was fickle with fickle weather, but there was never enough snow to make things wintry white. When the RV stopped, Elijah picked up some blankets as they exited the RV. Lynette paid little attention to how cold it was; she was too busy in awe of the blanket of white that surrounded her. She walked in Elijah's footsteps as they made their way to the observation area. There were several benches in which to sit on, and there were people already there in pitched tents with bonfires. It was like a classic winter scene with families roasting marshmallows and having smores as they waited for the appearance of the northern lights. Elijah and Lynette settled on a bench near the center of the observation space. He was careful to place blankets underneath, so the surface was not cold when Lynette sat down. He kept two blankets, one to drape across their shoulders and one to cover their laps.

"This is perfect," Lyn sighed.

"I'm kind of jealous of the folks with the smores," Elijah laughed.

"That does look like fun," Lynette agreed.

"Next time," Elijah responded. "Next time we'll have smores and a tent with hot cocoa."

"Or champagne," Lynette suggested.

"Champagne is a great option," Elijah concurred.

"Just knowing there is a next time even before the first time is over makes me a very happy girl," Lynette said as she accepted Elijah's loving arm around her.

And as though the Creator himself hit the light switch, the sky overhead began to light up. It was faint at first; a slight shading to the midnight blue of the sky and then more drastic and clearer as the billowy greens and lighter blues and even purples and brilliant reds began to dance across the expanse of God's heaven. It was miraculous and breathtaking and incredible all at the same time. Both Lynette and Elijah were rendered speechless as they lifted their collective heads towards the sky and absorbed all that was the northern lights that seemed to go on forever in spectacular waves.

"I can't even," Lynette whispered against the breeze that swirled around them.

"Me either," Elijah agreed.

They sat their together, amazed and in awe.

"Beautiful doesn't even describe it," Lynette sighed, momentarily lowering her gaze and turning her attention to Elijah. "I'm so full right now," Lynette confessed; her eyes soft and her head slightly tilted.

Elijah removed the glove from his hand and gently stroked the side of Lynette's face.

"And even with all this magnificence that we are bearing witness to, that we are experiencing together, the brilliance of this sky pales in comparison to the brilliance I see before me. You are one of God greatest creations, beloved."

SHE COULDN'T HELP but rest her head on Elijah's shoulder. What could she say to that? What words could she fine that were adequate enough to express what Lynette felt in her heart? In the absence of those words, Lynette nestled against Elijah, hoping that he felt her response move through him.

After a while, the couple got up from the bench they had been sitting on and took a stroll with the northern lights in the background. They had been holding hands, and Elijah paused when Lynette stopped, removing her hand from his. She bent down and with gloved hands, rolled snow together into a ball. When she stood up, Elijah saw what she was holding.

"Oh, is that what we're doing?"

"Mmhmm," Lynette hummed, hurling the snowball in Elijah's direction.

"Center mass, baby," Lynette squealed as she bent down to pick up another one. The cool swift chill she felt upon standing stopped her short as she was the recipient of Elijah's first snowball.

"Oh, it's on now!" Lynette exclaimed.

"Bring it on," Elijah challenged, kneeling and making another snowball. This time when he threw it, Lynette was watching, and side stepped his attack.

"Ah! You missed," Lynette roared with laughter, but Elijah was on to her, too, and moved out of the way of the next snowball she launched.

"That's it! You're mine now," Elijah rumbled, taking a step in Lyn' direction. But she had no intention of just standing there. Lynette struck out, jogging away from him, her feet slippery in the snow. She took a chance and looked over her shoulder, trying to gauge how close Elijah was. That was her fatal mistake because when she turned around, Elijah was right there. "Gotcha!"

Lynette giggled uncontrollably as Elijah lifted her from the ground and twirled her around, making her dizzy with the circles they made.

"Oh my God, Elijah! Put me down!"

"And if I don't?" Elijah asked, laughing himself.

"I don't know!" Lynette screamed with laughter.

"Idol threats," Elijah replied, sitting her down and holding her until her head stopped spinning.

"I had to say something," Lynette giggled.

"I bet you did," Elijah crooned, spinning Lynette in his hands.

"You stopped didn't you," Lynette teased.

"True," Elijah admitted.

"Then the threat wasn't so idol after all."

"You win," Elijah acquiesced.

"I'm winning because I'm with you."

"Now you're trying to steal my heart," Elijah strummed.

Lynette smiled and shrugged her shoulders. "Maybe."

They shared an intimate smile. Lynette laced her fingers into Elijah's as they strolled to their temporary home.

And when their night under the northern lights was over, Elijah and Lynette returned to the RV and spent the night wrapped in each other's arms. Lynette felt the same. She felt comforted.

12

Lynette woke up the next morning nestled against the man she said I love you to just hours before. The feeling was surreal, and she didn't regret uttering those powerful words. Even if Elijah hadn't said it first, Lynette had to acknowledge what was in her heart.

Lynette's heart; the one thing she felt betrayed her in the past, the one thing she vowed not to guide her actions in the future, she was listening to. But it didn't feel like betrayal or a fool's errand. Lynette felt love for Elijah past her heart. She knew it in her mind, and it echoed in her soul. Elijah rustled underneath her. Lynette didn't intend to wake him. She was just as content lying next to him, feeling him, listening to him breathe. Elijah rustled again. In doing so, he pulled Lynette in even closer, exhaling deeply and settling in. Lyn smiled. She felt right at home.

Lynette didn't realize she'd drifted off to sleep until she felt Elijah kissing her lightly on the neck, arousing her awake.

"Mmmm," Lynette moaned as Elijah's lips grazed her cheek.

"Don't do that," he whispered. Elijah was already aroused by her presence. But Lyn's verbal utterances sent a surge coursing through him that Elijah wasn't sure he could rein in. When she moaned again, Elijah could barely restrain himself. He didn't want to push her too soon to a place she might not be ready to go. Elijah didn't want to risk putting his own desires ahead of Lynette's well-being. Although she hadn't given him the whole story of her past failed relationships, he knew enough to know she was fragile, delicate. Pushing her too soon could cost Elijah in the long run, and he wasn't willing to risk that. But Lynette was caught up in her own whirlwind; feeling the press of Elijah's masculinity against her; hearing him pant against her neck. She was already caught up.

"What time do we have to leave," Lyn asked turning over slightly so she could see Elijah face to face.

"Whenever we get ready," Elijah sighed. "That's one of the benefits of having your own plane.

"You are a very successful man, aren't you Elijah? I guess I didn't really put it into perspective before, but you are wildly successful. You must be so proud of yourself."

"I try not to be," Elijah insisted. "Pride comes before a fall, and I don't want that to happen," Elijah admitted. "I do my best to stay rooted and grounded, never forgetting that it's so easy to go backwards, you know?"

"I wish I could say I did," Lynette confessed. "I haven't had that kind of monumental success in my life so I can't say that I relate on that level."

"But you are honest, and decent and loving and put the needs of others ahead of your own. That Ms. Jones, makes you wildly successful on a level most people never reach."

"You humble me," Lynette whispered.

"Just telling the truth," Elijah answered.

Lyn rested her head on Elijah's chest as he gently stroked her curly locs.

"And to think that you love somebody like me," Lynette

mused. That thought was really supposed to be internal, something she didn't say aloud. But she had.

"You are worthy of incredible love, Lynette, and don't you ever doubt that," Elijah reassured.

"Thank you for that, Elijah."

Lynette lifted herself high enough to kiss Elijah sweetly on the lips. "And since we don't have to rush, I think I'm going to climb into the shower if that's okay with you?"

"That's fine, Elijah replied, kissing Lyn on the forehead. "I'll be right here when you get back."

Lynette smiled and then lifted her frame from the bed. She traipsed on tiptoe around the bed and down the short hall way before reaching the bathroom door. Lynette reached for the handle and then paused.

"Elijah, do you have a shirt I can wear once I get out?" She wore a wicked grin that turned Elijah on.

"I'm sure I can come up with something," Elijah winked.

"Or maybe nothing," Elijah mumbled as Lynette closed the door behind her.

His manhood thumped hard. *Down boy,* Elijah cautioned himself. It wasn't that easy though. Elijah tried to think clean thoughts and then laughed at himself when he couldn't manage it. And then he heard the sound of water from the shower and Elijah's mind began to wander; specific to Lynette.

She stood in the shower and let the hot water run over her body. Steam rose from the enclosure as Lynette allowed her head to drop back, resting on her shoulders. The water traveled from the crown of her head and down her back. It was refreshing and soothing. Lynette smiled as she thought about the northern lights and then smile more when she thought about waking up next to Elijah. Hearing a distinctive click brought Lynette's head from its resting place. She could sense Elijah before she saw him. Lynette sensed his hesitation as he stood just inside the door.

Without hesitation, she allied his fears, opening the shower door and extending her hand. Lynette blinked back the water that threatened her eyes and waited for Elijah to accept her.

He exhaled and discarded the t-shirt and shorts he'd been wearing. He saw Lynette's invitation, but still, Elijah hesitated, just for a moment. When she felt his strong hand gently fold into hers, Lynette sighed as her heart raced in her chest. Elijah stepped into the shower, and their eyes met. Lynette took a step back, compelling Elijah forward without dropping her gaze. She felt the cool of the tiles against her back and gasped behind the unexpected. Elijah stepped forward catching Lynette on her gasp kissing her so sensually it snatched her remaining breath away. Elijah lifted Lyn's hands and pressed them against the wall eradicating any space that could exist between them. Lynette felt the thick of Elijah's thickness pressing against her belly. She panted, wantonly. It had been a long time since someone loved Lynette and made love to her.

She whimpered and once again her vocalizations caused an unreconcilable stir in Elijah's core he could not ignore. Slowly, he bent his knees enough to get underneath her. He lowered one hand and lifted Lynette's leg, placing Lyn's foot on his thigh. Lyn's body moaned in response to that touch alone; her jewel pulsing and contracting in titillating anticipation.

"Elijah, please," Lyn sighed her body begging to be filled by him.

His brows raised and his eyes begged the question.

"Please, babe, don't make me wait any longer," Lyn whimpered.

"I want you to be sure," Elijah sighed.

"I've never been more sure of anything in my li- "

Lyn's words were stopped in midsentence as Elijah slowly teased the lips of her mound with the tip of his throbbing member. Lyn's knees buckled, but he held her firm as he slowly pushed into her. Lynette whimpered loudly; a mix of pleasure and delightful pain. It had been so long Lyn was like a virgin. Her womanly walls were tight. The press against his swollen dick made Elijah groan as he slowly methodically pushed gently inside her. He felt Lynette's walls give into him. Elijah looked up into Lyn's eyes as he moved further inside her. Seeing her mouth open with no sound coming out. He needed to feel her lips and h seized her mouth exploring her with his probing tongue. Elijah pinned Lyn against the wall feeling her swollen nipples against his rock-hard chest.

Elijah stood up straight inside her; the pulse of his manhood thumping against her clit. He stayed there, feeling her folds encasing him, squeezing against him, assuaging his dick. Lyn couldn't breathe. She loved how Elijah felt inside her, and her body screamed for more. Burying her face in the curve of his neck, Lyn leveraged her weight against the wall and as he felt the rise of a heated climax surging between her thighs she bounced on his hardness, grinding her clit against the tip of his dick.

"Oh my god, Babe," she whined as her body convulsed and she rocked her pussy harder and faster, feeling all of him leaving no space inside her. Elijah locked his knees, and his thighs tightened as he let Lynette have her way with him. When her head dropped back on a long guttural scream, Elijah leaned in ravaging the length of her elegant neck. His gentle bite to her wet flesh sent an electrical current from her neck straight to her jewel, and Lyn bounced harder and faster until she lost all sense of rhyme and reason. Elijah reached down and cupped Lynette's plump ass as her jewel took him in to the hilt.

"AHHHHH!!" She screamed; her head flailing from side to side as the first powerful wave of orgasm streaked through her. He felt her essence spilling onto him in a mighty rush. Elijah held on as long as he could to make sure Lynette got everything, she needed from him, but her pussy contracting and releasing and seizing up again was more than he could take. Elijah couldn't hold back anymore.

Ugh, bae, Rrrggghhhh," he groaned as his body took over, spilling his hot seed between her thighs.

Lynette collapsed onto him; her arms landing around Elijah's neck. Their jagged breathing was in sync as their bodies heaved and sighed in unison. Still, Lynette couldn't breathe. She felt all choked up, and she just couldn't get enough air into her lungs. Elijah felt her body shaking against his, and he held her tight.

You okay, babe," Elijah asked softly.

She didn't answer right away. She couldn't.

"Babe," Elijah repeated, leaning back and encouraging Lyn to look at him. Haltingly, Lynette lifted her head. Elijah could see the furrow in her brow and her eyes misted over that had nothing to do with the warm shower.

"I'm just," she started and then hesitated as hot tears pressed against the backs of her eyes. "I'm just so full right now," she stuttered as the tears began to fall.

Lyn rested her head on Elijah's shoulders as a well of emotions bubbled up inside her and spilled over. He held her. He didn't question her. Elijah let Lyn feel what she needed to feel. They stood there together as the water pounded against their flesh. Elijah was willing to stand there for as long Lynette needed. When Lynette lifted her head again the tears had stopped falling. Elijah found her eyes and they shared a warm smile. Lyn reached over and turned off the water. Elijah stepped out first retrieving a towel for her. When Lyn stepped out of the shower, he gently wiped away the beads of water that rested on her skin. When he was done, he helped Lynette wrap the towel around her. She helped him get dry, gently running the heated towel over Elijah's handsomely chiseled face, across the breath of his shoulders and down the length of his center. She watched as he wrapped and knotted the towel around his waist.

"I hope I didn't ruin it for you," Lyn offered. Unsure of how Elijah would take her tears.

"You could never do that unless you stopped liking me," he smiled.

"I more than like you," Lyn smiled.

"I more than like you, too."

🎜 13 🎜

They exited the bathroom hand in hand.

"I'm so hungry," Lynette admitted as she sat on the edge of the bed.

"Me too," Elijah smiled. "Let me see what we have in the kitchen."

"I can do that," Lynette suggested.

"No, you just relax. I've got this."

"Okay, then," Lynette sighed. She stretched out across the bed and laid on her stomach crossing her feet at the ankle. It was like watching Elijah walk down her sidewalk; that same smooth swagger as he strolled down the length of the RV to the kitchenette. Without even realizing it, Lynette had lifted her legs at the knee and was waving her feet in the air like a school girl. He made her so happy; dangerously happy. If he hurt her, it would be so painful, but Lynette had already jumped in with both feet. She had dived off the cliff with no parachute. There was no use in turning back now. She didn't want to; not in her mind her heart nor her soul.

God, please let him be good to me, Lyn thought as she watched Elijah lean over as he opened the refrigerator. Before long, the RV was filled with wonderful smells that made Lynette's stomach growl. She was glad Elijah didn't hear it. Lifting herself from the bed Lynette padded down the hallway, easing up behind Elijah as he scrambled eggs in a black cast iron skillet. Lyn laced her fingers around his waist.

"You look like you know what you're doing," Lynette mused as she rested her head on Elijah's expansive back.

"I can do a little something something." Elijah turned off the eye of the stove and set the skillet down. He turned on his heels, lifting his arm to embrace Lynette as he went. He reached across the counter and picked up a fork. Lifting some of the eggs onto the fork, Elijah leaned down and blew against the eggs causing steam to rise.

"Taste," he encouraged raising the fork to her lips. He watched as Lynette opened her mouth and slid the eggs off the fork. Lynette's eyes lifted as she chewed.

"Mmmm, Elijah, these are good."

He smiled and fed Lynette, enjoying the fact that she was enjoying his food. When the skillet was nearly empty, Elijah reached into the refrigerator and pulled out orange juice. He poured Lynette a glass and then poured a glass for himself. They drank, each eying the other over the top of their glasses. It was magnetic and perceivably innocent. But between Elijah and Lynette, it was a salacious tease. He couldn't resist, and Elijah didn't try. He eased in front of her sitting down his glass and removing the glass from Lynette's hand. This time when he kissed her, Lynette felt his animalistic craving taking her mouth and devouring her.

"Elijah," she panted between heated kisses.

As if hearing his name triggered a spike in Elijah's sexual desire, he began to devour Lynette, his manhood pressing hard against her. If there was any trepidation or hesitancy, Lynette was finding it more and more difficult to hold, she didn't have a desire to. Elijah awakened something in her that she wasn't sure could be silenced with fear and insecurity.

Elijah peeled Lynette's towel from her and allowed it to

drop carelessly to the floor. She called his name again. Lynette's body continued to give way under his persuasive touch. Lynette felt Elijah's strong hands pulling her closer in to him. She saw the desire in his eyes and felt the weight of it pressing firmly against her. Elijah released her briefly; long enough to drop the towel from around his waist. Elijah didn't want his hands away from Lynette for longer than absolutely necessary.

Lynette was struck by the flex of Elijah's muscular chest and the ripples of his well-articulated shoulders as he discarded the towel leaving his chest and his body bare. Again, their eyes met, and Lynette's emotions were caught up in the rapture of everything she physically felt. Lynette inhaled as the nip of the air exaggerated the tautness of her plump nipples. She inhaled again as Elijah's mouth covered them, one then the other. The heat that rose between Lynette's thighs made her legs quiver.

"Elijah," she whispered, panting hard.

The surge of hot heat that flowed through Lynette was hard to contain as he touched her in a special way. As Elijah fondled her sweetness, the carnal pressure between the two left no room for anything except succumbing to the overwhelming sensations layering one on top of the other. After pleasuring Lynette digitally and bringing the first of her pearls' nectar to bear, Elijah's eyes met hers. There was a moment of absolute clarity when Lynette knew that she wanted to give everything she had available, mentally, emotionally, physically and soulfully to Elijah. His eyes reflected the same; his desire to be with her and her alone.

Elijah took Lynette in his arms and lavished her with deep, penetrating kisses. Elijah eased the tip of his hardened cock inside her welcoming folds, the arch of her foot resembled a ballerina's point. Lynette's vaginal walls pulsed as Elijah eased his girth inside her. Her body's response of sweet nectar smoothed the way as he slowly pushed the width and breadth of his nine inches to the top of her jewel.

"Ahh…" Lynette moaned as the walls of her jewel contracted and released to accept her lover inside. It didn't hurt as much when he entered her, but still, the pain was a wonderfully aching pain that Lynette eagerly endured. Soon, the two fell into a nice rhythm, slow and methodical; the giver and receiver feeling equal. Elijah bent his knees gaining leverage as he thrust harder and deeper inside Lynette. He held on to the counter, one hand on each side as he pumped; the muscles in his long mahogany legs constricting and tensing.

Elijah groaned as he grabbed Lynette's curvaceous ass. His grip heightened Lynette's sensibilities as Elijah thrust deeper.

"Shit," Elijah groaned on the verge of climax. Elijah grabbed Lynette by the waist and moved inside her to the hilt inside her giving walls.

"Elijah, oh my, mmm, Elijah…" Lynette was absolutely breathless as her full breasts rocked back and forth in time with each thrust from Elijah's dick. She too was on the verge of explosion as her body spasmed from the lovely pounding he was giving her. The pace in which Elijah's hips thrust forward coupled with the slapping sound of his thighs meeting hers heightened the explosion the two shared together. Lynette released a wave of hot wetness as her body convulsed with pleasure. Elijah loved her through his climax and continued to thrust at a slower pace until all the gism he had to offer was expelled and Lyn's body stopped quaking. Although, Elijah enjoyed that part. It meant Lynette enjoyed him; her body enjoyed him.

"Ahhh," Lynette sighed and then smiled. "Elijah," she purred.

"Beautiful, when you call my name like that, it does something to me."

An easy and lusty smile tipped the corners of Lynette's lips. "I know."

"Alright then," Elijah crooned. "Be warned."

"Because the cat's out of the bag now?" Lynette taunted.

"Something like that."

He reached for her, pulling Lynette in to a warm hug. Their bodies rocked slowly as they made more than a physical connection. It was in that quiet moment that they bonded with their heartbeats their thoughts and aspirations for the future. And after another hot shower, Elijah and Lynette climbed into bed and slept, cuddled together.

"It's hard to leave," Lynette said as they boarded the jet.

"We'll be back," Elijah replied as he buckled Lyn's seatbelt.

"That does make leaving a little easier," Lyn smiled. "Everything about this trip has been amazing. You, Elijah, have been amazing."

"My amazing is a mere reflection of your amazing," Elijah replied.

The captain's voice registered over the intercom. "Take off will be in fifteen minutes."

"I already regret going home" Lynette sighed.

"Why is that?"

"Because," Lynette groaned, "work tomorrow."

Elijah wrapped his arm around Lynette's shoulders. "We don't have to think about that now," Elijah encouraged. "We don't have to think about work until tomorrow."

"What do you suggest we think about, with an emphasis on we," Lynette giggled.

"Hmm, anything but work," Elijah replied.

"We can talk about your work," Lynette suggested, turning in to face him. "It's definitely more exciting than the mailroom. So, what amazing project are you working on?"

"Uhn uhn," Elijah grumbled. "No work, not even mine."

"Fine," Lynette playfully fussed. "I just feel like there are still some very important things I don't know about you."

"I'm an open book. You can ask me anything you want, but no work," Elijah reminded.

"No work," Lynette agreed.

"So, what do you want to know?"

"Tell me about your family, outside of Uncle Bobby, who I adore, by the way."

"Uncle Bobby is kind of adorable," Elijah smiled.

"Yes, he is," Lynette chimed. "And we have to go back to his restaurant because those shrimp and grits? To die for."

"He already asked when you would be coming back," Elijah chortled.

"He did?" Lynette asked curiously.

Elijah's lips took on a pouty slant as he shook his head.

"You are the first woman I've taken to Uncle Bobby's restaurant, probably since my college days."

"I find that hard to believe," Lyn replied.

"Actually, it's true," Elijah answered. "I just hadn't run into anyone that I wanted to meet my uncle. That is, before you."

Lynette's cheeks flushed warmly. "He's that important to you, huh?"

"He is," Elijah replied. "Uncle Bobby is like a surrogate father to me. We, my brother and I had my dad, but because of the kind of work he did, dad couldn't always be around. My dad was in the military, and so he would be gone for long stretches of time. Uncle Bobby stepped in to make sure our mom felt supported when dad was away. He did all the daddy stuff with us, baseball practice, getting our chores done, and made sure we were straight until our father could come home. And it didn't matter what it was that we might have needed, Uncle Bobby made sure we had it, every single time."

"That's a powerful testament," Lynette replied.

"It is. He's a great man," Elijah continued. "Uncle Bobby didn't have kids of his own, so I guess we were his surrogate sons, in more ways than one. So, the fact that I brought you to the restaurant put all kinds of thoughts in the old man's head," Elijah laughed. "He's convinced that if I brought you to meet him; not to eat the food, but to meet him, then there must be something extra special about you."

"I knew I liked Uncle Bobby," Lyn guffawed.

"Well he certainly likes you," Elijah seconded.

They felt the rev of the jet. Elijah reached for Lynette's hand as the jet began taxiing down the runway and didn't release it until the jet leveled off.

"You have a brother? I didn't know that," Lyn continued.

"I do, an older brother by a few years, Emmanuel."

"Are you too close?"

"We are," Elijah answered. "But E never let's me forget that he's the big brother," Elijah paused. "Emmanuel is a psychology professor at Morehouse seeking tenure. He thinks he's so smart," Elijah snarked.

"You call him, E? That's cute," Lynette laughed. "And he probably is smart; much like his younger, more handsome brother," Lyn teased.

"We are all E's," Elijah scoffed. "I guess my mom and dad thought it was cute. They used to tell the story that they thought it was kismet that they found each other, and both their first names began with E. My dad? Ezra. My mom? Evelyn."

"That is totally cute," Lynette smiled. "I love it."

"Okay, enough about me," Elijah said. "Tell me about your family?"

"Hmm, let's see," Lynette began. "You already know Samantha is like the sister I never had. Part of that is because I don't actually have a sister," Lyn laughed. "I have a brother, younger by a few years, who I absolutely love and adore and can't stand at the same time. And I act like the overbearing big sister, and it drives him nuts which makes me completely ecstatic."

"You, overbearing? I can't imagine," Elijah scoffed.

Lyn reached over and punched Elijah in the arm. He feigned injury, grabbing his arm and massaging as though it hurt.

"Stop! Don't even try it," Lynette grinned.

"And your parents?" Elijah asked.

"Malcolm and Stephanie Jones," Lynette said proudly. "They live in Florida, trying to play like they are retired. My dad constantly fidgeting because he's a workaholic and Florida was mom's idea, and mom driving him nuts reminding him that they are supposed to be retired and relaxing."

"They sound wonderful," Elijah mused.

"They are," Lynette replied. "They are good people."

Lynette adjusted on the couch, turning fully toward Elijah. "Would you say your parents are happily married?"

"I would say yes," Elijah replied. "My mom is strong, always has been. She loved my dad, and his absences only seemed to make mom love him more. When dad came back, he was a good dad and a good husband. So yeah, I would say they are happily married."

"Hmm," Lynette hummed.

"What, beautiful? I can see your wheels turning?" Elijah observed.

I don't know," Lynette began, positioning her elbow on the arm of the couch until her head rested on her hand. "Don't you think it's interesting that our parents have had happy marriages, yet..."

"Yet," Elijah repeated, "neither of us has?"

"Yes," Lynette answered. "I may only be speaking for me, but I saw a great example of what love looks like, but love, lasting two directional love still seemed to elude me," Lyn mused.

"Why do you think that is?"

"Hmph," Lyn huffed. "I never really thought about it like this," Lynette shook her head. "I think I wanted what my parents had so bad that I loved hard; too hard with people that clearly didn't love me."

"Or didn't deserve the kind of love you had to offer," Elijah added.

"Yeah, maybe so," Lynette sighed.

The duo fell silent as they both contemplated.

"What about you, Elijah?"

"I think there is a part of me that wanted to emulate what my parents had, minus the long absences. I saw what that did to my mother, and I wouldn't want to put the woman that I love through that. Even with the absences, though, my father loved my mother, and when he was home, he took great care of her. That's the art I think I was drawn too; the look in my mother's eyes when her man was at home." Elijah paused and then continued. "I wanted someone to look at me like my mom looks at my dad. It's funny though. When there was that look, I couldn't seem to trust that it was genuine; that she was looking at me in that way because she truly loved me. I was suspicious of that look and as a result, disconnected from it because I didn't trust it."

Elijah's honesty was refreshing and pricked Lyn's heart because she found it easy to be honest with him; another first.

"Do you think you will ever trust that look; the one you've

been waiting for?" Lyn's question was tentative, but she really wanted to know.

"Without question," Elijah responded affirmatively. Elijah unbuckled his seatbelt and moved closer to Lynette, easing her head from her hand and taking it into his own. "When you look at me, beloved, I see the purity of your gaze; not because of what I have. You didn't know enough about me the first time we met for you to have any preconceived notions about me. Still, that pure, honest, unfiltered look was there. It was hopeful and curious about who I am as a man. It's the same way my mom looks at my dad. She still looks at him with hope and curiosity after all these years, like there is still something intriguing about him, something she can learn with him."

Lynette inclined her head to the fullness of Elijah's gentle hand. The words that poured from his lips were enough to make her heart swell. They were like salve gently coating a wound that never seemed to heal. She did feel curious and hopeful when she looked at Elijah. He felt it. He saw it, too.

"We will be landing in cool but sunny Atlanta in just a few minutes," the captain said.

"Uh," Lynette moaned. "That means it's over."

"Just this trip is over, beautiful, just this trip," Elijah reminded. "I'm not going anywhere unless you want me to."

"Don't play with me, Elijah Sinclair," Lynette sniped.

"I won't," he laughed. "You can't get rid of me now, even if you wanted to."

"And I don't," Lyn smiled.

The jet landed successfully and soon after, Lynette and Elijah were wisked away from the airport on the way to her home.

"This date was incredible," Lynette sighed. "Thank you, Elijah."

"Anytime and always," Elijah replied.

They arrived at Lynette's home faster than she would have liked.

All good things must come to an end, she thought. Despite Elijah's reassurance, Lynette hoped it was just a temporary end.

Once the car was parked, Elijah took her by the hand. The moment their fingers touched, and she felt the warmth of his outstretched hand, Lyn felt comforted reassurance that this wasn't the last time. Elijah walked Lynette to the door and waited until she opened it and stepped inside.

"I guess you're not going to close the door," Elijah flushed.

"Nope," Lyn smiled. "Not until I watch your sexy ass walk away."

She loved the look of embarrassment on his face as he took that first trepidatious step down the walkway.

"Elijah," Lynette called after.

He pivoted on his heels, and she saw the flushed smile on his face.

"Text me when you get home. Let me know you're safe, okay?"

"Will do," he smiled. Elijah backpedaled a few steps watching Lynette watching him.

"Gone on, turn around," Lynette teased. "Don't deprive me."

He didn't. Elijah strolled away confidently, whether that was intentional or not.

Lynette was still floating on a cloud when she finally closed her front door. Work would be tomorrow, but work would have to wait. For the moment, Lynette was happy, and she would be even happier once she heard from Elijah.

"Come on Lyn, answer the phone."

Samantha was absolutely vibrating.

"Lyn please, answer."

"Babe," Samantha said, turning to her husband. "I don't think this is a good idea. She doesn't need to find out like this. I should go to her."

"Hello?"

Shit, Samantha cursed covering the speaker of the phone.

Lance placed a loving hand to Samantha's back, encouraging her to respond. She had no choice at this point.

"Lyn hey it's Sam."

"Samantha, I didn't hear the phone. I was in the ladies. What's up?"

"Lyn, I don't want you to get upset, but I have to tell you something."

Lynette sat down, slowly on her bed. Hearing Samantha say that she didn't want her to be upset was upsetting. It felt like one of those early morning phone calls; the kind that comes before the sun rises. The kind of call that you know is bad, even before you pick up the phone because who calls at that time of morning, unless it is bad news. It's always bad news.

"What's the matter?"

Samantha hated this. She could hear it in Lyn's voice. Yet, Samantha knew all too well what being on the other end of the line in a situation like this must have felt like. She just had to say it.

"There's been an accident."

"An accident?" Lynette's heart was beating hard in her chest, and she felt adrenaline jutting through her veins. There was a sinking feeling in her gut.

"Yes, Lynette. We just got the call. Elijah's been in an accident. Lance and I are on the way to the hospital. We can come by and pick you up."

"Elijah?" Lynette jumped to her feet. Instantly she felt sick to her stomach. "Oh my God, is he okay? What hospital? Is Elijah okay?"

"Let us come and pick you up. We can go to the hospital together."

"Samantha! Is Elijah okay??"

"I don't know all the details, sweetie. I'm so sorry."

"What hospital did they take him to?" Lyn demanded.

"Grady," Samantha answered. "Lyn, we can be there in a few minutes. We'll go to"

Samantha drew back from the phone as she heard the line go dead in her hand.

"She hung up on me," Sam sighed.

"Driver," Lance commanded, "get us to Ms. Jones' place, immediately."

"Yes, sir."

"It will be okay, babe, I promise," Lance replied, turning his attention to Samantha.

"I'm worried Lance," Samantha whimpered.

"I know." Lance pulled Samantha into his arms and held her.

Lynette was distraught and absolutely beside herself. Elijah promised that he was going to call or text her to let her know he was safe. Elijah didn't call. He broke his promise to Lynette. He didn't call or text to tell her he was safe. She couldn't think. Her nerves were shot. Lyn was pacing. She called Elijah's phone and waited for him to pick up. It went to voicemail.

He never sends me to voicemail, Lynette thought. Her hands started to shake as the realization set in. Her eyes were already filled with tears that threatened to fall. She couldn't breathe again, but for all the wrong reasons. Elijah was in a car accident. She didn't know how bad, but Elijah was hurt. Lynette pulled the Lyft app up on her phone as she made her way to the front door. The sickening churning in her stomach continued. She had to get to Elijah; she just had to.

LANCE AND SAMANTHA pulled up to Lynette's house. Lance jumped out of the car and ran to the front door. He didn't wait for the driver to do so. This was important. He had to do it himself. Lance rang the doorbell and knocked on the door simultaneously. He peered through the side panel trying to see if Lynette was there and then knocked again. Samantha looked on anxiously, praying that Lynette was there, that she waited for them. This was not something Sam wanted her best friend to try and handle on her own. She needed to be there for Lynette, like Lyn had been there so many times for her. She craned her neck trying to see if Lance got a response. When he turned back towards the car, alone, Samantha wasn't completely surprised. Lynette wasn't there. She left without them.

Lance trekked back towards the car and climbed in.

"I'm sorry, babe," Lance said closing the door.

"It's not your fault," Samantha replied. She was worried. Lance could see it in Samantha's eyes and in the wringing of her hands.

Driver, Grady hospital."

"Yes, sir."

"COME ON, come on, please get their fast."

Those were Lynette's thoughts as she sat in the back of the Lyft. Her utterance was not intended to be spoken aloud, but she did speak them aloud. The driver didn't take offense though. She could see the distress on her passenger's face. Lynette couldn't settle. She didn't know what to do with herself. All she could think about was getting to Elijah. And it was taking too fucking long. The traffic in Atlanta was getting in Lynette's way, keeping her from him when all she wanted was to get to Elijah. She wanted to curse and scream and demand that everybody get out of her gottdamn way. She wanted to blare the horn and make them move. But she couldn't do that. All she could do was hope that traffic moved favorably so she could get to Elijah. Lynette swiped at the tears that continued to stain her cheeks.

Elijah, please be okay…

Whether that was a plea to the Creator or the outcry from a heart that was breaking, Lynette continued to be anxious, looking out of the passenger side window, looking ahead to the traffic in front of her. When the Lyft driver finally exited the interstate, Lynette's heart started to beat faster. That meant she was getting closer to seeing about Elijah. Thankfully Grady Hospital wasn't far from the interstate, and within minutes, the car was pulling up to the emergency room door.

"Thank you," Lynette called out as she quickly exited the back of the car. her feet couldn't get to the emergency room door fast enough. Lynette only had one thing on her mind. She impatiently waited as the automated emergency room doors opened. Lynette started off walking fast but then she was running, down the hallway, apologizing for bumping into people who had nothing to do with her emergency.

"Elijah Sinclair," Lynette panted, finally reaching the nurses' station. "Where is Elijah Sinclair?"

Her voice was urgent and demanding.

"Are you family?"

"What? I need to know what happened to Elijah Sinclair, ma'am please. Where is he," Lynette insisted.

"I understand you are concerned ma'am," the nurse

replied. "But unless your family, I can't disclose whether Mr. Sinclair is even a patient here."

Lynette was befuddled. "Please, I need to know if he's here? Please!"

"I'm sorry, ma'am."

Even after the nurse apologetically walked away, all Lynette could do was stand there. All she wanted to do is get to Elijah, and now she was stalled; unsure of what to do next.

"Lynette?"

She almost didn't hear her name being called over the noise natural to the emergency room.

"Lyn," Samantha said again this time finally reaching her friend and placing her hands gently on Lynette's shoulders.

When Lynette came out of the fog, her brow wrinkled first, and then her lips started to quiver. Then tears began to fall afresh from Lynette's red-tinged eyes. Samantha's brow wrinkled in response as she pulled Lynette into her, consoling her.

"Sam," Lynette cried, "they won't tell me anything, nothing."

Samantha held Lynette as her friend's body shook in her arms. Sam's eyes traveled to her husband. She communicated without words. Lance nodded as he understood the nonverbal communication that existed between husband and wife. Lance walked with authority to the nurses' station.

Samantha attended to Lynette. She was confident Lance would handle the nurse.

"Why won't they tell me anything," Lynette moaned. "Does that mean he's dead since they won't let me see him? Please, Samantha, tell me he's not dead?"

"That's not why," Lynette. "You've got to have faith that Elijah is still with us."

"But they won't talk to me. They won't tell me anything," she cried. "I know I'm not his family, but Sam, I care about him, a lot. I need to know he's okay."

"I know, Lyn," Samantha sighed. "I know."

Lance walked away from the nurses' station and stood behind Samantha. Lynette looked up into Lance's face as she separated from Samantha. Lynette wanted to be hopeful, looking into Lance's eyes. But all she felt was hopelessness and despair.

"I'm sorry it took a minute, but when you're ready Lynette, we can go to the third floor," Lance replied.

Her drawback was slow, and her eyes were wide.

"He's?"

"Elijah is in surgery, right now, but we can go upstairs and wait for him," Lance replied.

Lynette's eyes traveled to Samantha's and then back to Lance's. It wasn't clear that what Lance said fully registered. Samantha stepped in, wrapping her arm around Lyn's waist.

"Come on, Lyn. Let's go see about Elijah."

Lance moved to the other side of Lynette, and he and Samantha encamped around her. When she was ready to move, they all moved in unison towards the elevators. The ride to the third floor was quiet. Lynette had stopped crying, but Samantha could still feel Lyn's body shivering next to her. When the elevator door dinged, Lynette froze as the door opened. Elijah being in the hospital, being in surgery all became very real.

"It's okay, Lyn," Samantha whispered. "We are right here with you."

There was a part of Lynette that wanted to rush from the elevator, to run to Elijah's side. Yet, there was another part of Lynette that was frightened; that was scared to find out what was going on with Elijah. What if he was dead and they just didn't want to tell her? What if they were waiting until they were in a less crowded space to break the terrible news to her? What if he was so badly hurt that he would never be the same; the same Elijah that Lynette had come to know and love? The thought of any of that was exacerbating and overwhelming, and it kept Lynette's feet from moving despite what Samantha said. The elevator started to buzz as the doors threatened to close. Samantha urged Lynette on. She and Lance compelled Lyn's feet to move. Lance held his hand over the door to make sure they were all off the elevator before the doors closed.

"Babe why don't you and Lynette go to the waiting room. I will talk to the nurses."

Samantha shook her head and guided Lynette to the waiting area. They were both slow to sit but doing what Lance suggested was best.

Lance kept his emotions in check. This was not the time to allow how he felt about Elijah's situation to rise to the surface. His wife and her best friend were counting on Lance to be strong. He had to be that for them.

"Excuse me," Lance said clearing his throat.

"Yes, may I help you," a nurse replied.

"I'm trying to check on the status of Elijah Sinclair."

"Give me just a moment, okay?"

The nurse turned away from Lance and walked over to a computer. He hated waiting and wondering. Silently Lance prayed for good news. When the nurse turned and started walking in his direction, Lance couldn't deny how anxious he felt.

"Mr. Sinclair is still in surgery," the nurse began. "Dr. Flemings is his surgeon and will come out and speak with you as soon as possible."

"Okay, but can you tell me anything about his condition? Was he seriously hurt?" Lance pressed.

"I'm sorry, sir," the nurse replied. "I'm not at liberty to say. But as soon as the surgeon is available, I will send him right out."

That's the best she could do. That was the most could tell her. It didn't satisfy Lance's need to know, but it was the best she could do. That wasn't her fault. Lance strolled to the waiting room. All he could tell Samantha and Lynette is what he knew, which wasn't much. But that's all Lance knew. That's all he could tell them. It would have to be enough.

❦ 15 ❦

FOUR HOURS LATER

"I can't stand this! This waiting, this not knowing," Lynette bemoaned. "What are they doing to him? Why hasn't anyone told us anything?"

Lynette had paced the floor as much as she could stand. She had sat in the hard waiting room chair as long as she could. Although Lance had recently come back from the nurses' station trying to solicit information, they still didn't know anything. It was getting to be too much.

"Hopefully it won't be too much longer," Samantha reasoned.

"Do either of you want something to drink," Lance offered. He felt useless, waiting and watching for the surgeon. The least he could do is get coffee.

"No, babe I'm good," Samantha sighed, reaching out and taking Lance's hand.

"Lynette?"

"No, I'm okay, Lance, thank you."

Lance wasn't the only one who felt useless. They all did, to some degree.

When the door that separated the waiting room from the surgical wing opened, they all turned in that direction. When a man in green scrubs walked out, removing the mask from his face as he did, they all stood up.

"You are the family for Mr. Sinclair," the doctor asked.

"Yes," Lynette replied, stepping close to Samantha and reaching for her hand. Samantha folded hers over Lyn's. Lynette's heart felt like it was dropping out of the place it was supposed to be; moving down to her churning gut. She was nervous and anxious and couldn't read the doctor's face. She didn't know whether it was good news or bad news because she couldn't read the surgeon's face. Lynette wanted to search his eyes for the answer, but fear got the best of her; choking her from clarity.

"I'm Dr. Fleming," the surgeon replied.

"How's he doing, doctor," Lance said, stepping forward. Lance found himself struggling with the same thing Lynette did, seeking an answer in the doctor's presentation.

"Mr. Sinclair is stable," Dr. Fleming began.

Samantha felt Lyn buckle next to her. She immediately wrapped her arms around Lynette's waist, holding her up. Lynette was overwhelmed with a rush of emotions. But she had to pull herself together to hear what more the doctor had to say.

"What happened, Dr. Fleming," Lance asked.

"It appears that a driver traveling in the opposite direction ran a red light. Fortunately for Mr. Sinclair, the driver was attentive and quick and turned the car so as the side of Mr. Sinclair's vehicle sustained much of the impact. In doing so, the chauffer probably saved both their lives. Mr. Sinclair ended up requiring surgery because when the glass from the passenger side window broke, he sustained a serious laceration to his left side, as well as other punctures and lacerations from glass shards."

The doctor spoke very matter of factly, but he didn't speak in a way that was unclear. He was very clear and straight-forward.

"How is Elijah doing?" Lynette asked, reengaging in the conversation. She had to know. Elijah promised he was going to let her know he was safe. He didn't keep his promise. She would forgive Elijah for that as long as he was okay. She would fuss at Elijah later. For now, Lyn had to know how he was doing.

"Mr. Sinclair is stable, ma'am."

Lynette breathed an audible sigh of relief. Still, Lynette couldn't keep her body from shaking or her heart from pounding uncontrollably in her chest. Samantha and Lance felt relieved, too. "He was heavily sedated during the surgery, so he's resting," Dr. Fleming continued. "You should be able to see him in a few minutes once he is settled into his room."

"Thanks so much, Dr. Fleming," Lance replied, offering his hand.

"You're most welcome."

"Feel better," Samantha asked as she turned to Lynette.

"It's good to know he's stable," Lyn answered just above a whisper. It was really all she could manage.

Samantha watched as Lyn's eyes clouded with tears once more.

"He's going to be okay, Lynette," Samantha said, reaffirming the grip she had on Lyn's hands. "Elijah is going to be okay."

Lyn managed to squeeze Samantha's hand, but then she let it go. Samantha watched as Lynette walked quickly out of the waiting area, disappearing around a corner. Samantha started after her.

"Let her go, Sam" Lance suggested, reaching out and catching Samantha by the waist. "Give her a minute."

Samantha looked to the hallway again. She wanted to chase after Lynette to make sure she was okay. But looking back at Lance, she knew he might be right. Lynette probably needed a minute alone. And she did. Lynette burst through the ladies' room door. By the time she reached the vanity

Lynette's hands were shaking so bad she needed to hold on to the counter just to try and steady herself. She breathed out long and slow, through her mouth; trying to regulate her erratic heart beat and maybe quiet the horribly chaotic rumble in her gut. She heard the sound before she realized it emanated from her mouth. It was a horrible, sharp, high-pitched wail that came from all the uncertainty, and worry, and stress Lynette had been under. Once Lynette realized it was her making the noise, she raised a hand to her mouth to quiet herself.

Lynette raised her head and saw her reflection in the mirror. She looked haggard; her eyes were swollen and red. She couldn't see Elijah looking like that. She shook her head at how ridiculous that thought was. Reaching over, Lynette turned on the water, allowing it to warm. Lynette ran her fingers under the water gauging the temperature, and when it was lukewarm, Lynette bent down and splashed water onto her face. Lynette found a paper towel and patted her face dry. She continued to look in the mirror at her reflection centering herself as she smoothed out her hair. After another deep breath, Lynette turned from the mirror. She needed to see Elijah. Lynette needed to see him for herself to know he was okay.

Even though Samantha agreed with what Lance suggested, she couldn't help looking over her shoulder to see when Lynette was coming back. She was tempted to get up and go check, just to make sure. Samantha looked over her shoulder once last time and was relieved to see Lynette making her way towards them. At about the same time, the door next to the nurses' station opened and hearing that, Lynette pivoted on her heels. It only took a few seconds before Sam and Lance were standing by her side.

"Is everything okay," Lynette asked.

"Yes," a nurse replied. "You can see Mr. Sinclair now if you'd like. He's in room 316."

"Thank you," Lance replied.

The nurse smiled and turned back towards the door.

"Are you ready, Lyn," Samantha asked.

Lynette nodded, feeling another wave of strong emotion rush over her. Even though the doctor reassured her that Elijah was stable, Lynette was still nervous to see him. Her eyes traveled to each placard as they made their way down the hall; 312, 313, 314. The trio arrived at room 316 and Lance pushed the door open. Samantha was the first to enter with Lynette a few steps behind. Lyn didn't notice when Lance entered as she was immediately transfixed by what she heard first and then saw. As Lynette stepped from behind Sam, her ears were pricked by the variety of beeps and noises of the machines that surrounded Elijah's bed. Her eyes slowly traveled from the machinery to the bed. She saw the white sheet that covered his legs, the monitor attached to his finger and the bandage covering the IV needle stuck in his arm. Then, Lynette's eyes traveled the length of his arm across his chest, up the length of him until her eyes rested on Elijah's face. His eyes were closed, and as Lynette stepped forward, she looked at his chest again and stared to see if she could see his chest rise and fall. She heard the monitors that said he was alive, but Lynette watched to see for herself the rise and fall of Elijah's chest. It was only after she saw the sheet that covered him move up and down more than once did Lynette exhale the breath, she didn't even realize she was holding.

Lance and Samantha positioned themselves on either side of the bed, leaving the spot right next to Elijah for Lynette. She was slow to approach him even though Lynette was relieved to see him, to see that he was alive and breathing.

Thank God he's okay," Samantha uttered. "Hurt but okay."

Lynette placed her hand on the rail of the bed. Her eyes remained fixed on Elijah.

"I'm sure he'll sleep for a while," Lance observed. He was

relieved that his boy was okay. Samantha quietly padded over to where Lance stood and wrapped her arm around his waist. She knew how much Elijah meant to Lance. This was hard on him, too.

"He probably will," Samantha replied.

They stayed by Elijah's beside for a few hours watching him. Nurses came and went. They checked the machines and Elijah's IV site. They wrote on the clipboard at the foot of the bed. Dr. Fleming came in before the end of his shift. He checked the notes they had written and then checked on his patient.

"Mr. Sinclair's vitals look good," Dr. Fleming advised.

"Is he supposed to be sleeping this long," Lynette asked.

"It's not uncommon," Dr. Fleming replied. "Some individuals have a greater sleep response to the anesthesia. But we will continue to monitor him through the night." Dr. Fleming continued. "If there are no more questions, I bid you all good night. We'll take good care of Mr. Sinclair, okay?"

They all nodded and thanked the doctor.

"Sam, Lance, if you guys want to go," Lynette began. "I'm gonna stay for a while."

"Are you sure, Lyn? Because we will stay with you and Elijah as long as you need us to," Samantha replied.

"I'm sure," Lyn replied.

Samantha rounded the bed with Lance just a few steps behind her.

"If you need anything, if Elijah needs anything, we are just a phone call away."

Samantha opened her arms, and Lynette stepped in for a hug.

"Love you, Sam, thank you."

"Girl you know you don't have to thank me. We love you and Elijah."

Samantha stepped back enough for Lance to wrap his arm around Lynette's shoulder.

"You'll call when he wakes up?"

"Absolutely," Lyn answered. "And thanks for everything Lance."

"No worries," Lance replied. "I took the liberty of contacting Elijah's family to let them know about the accident. They'll probably drive up tomorrow."

"What about Bishop, Elijah's driver," Lyn asked.

"Minor cuts and scrapes from what the nurse said," Lance explained. "They are keeping him for observation but expect he will be released."

"That's a blessing," Lynette sighed. "I'll make sure to tell Elijah when he wakes up."

Lynette watched as Samantha and Lance exited the room. It was just her and Elijah. The room suddenly felt very quiet. Lynette turned back to the bed. She hadn't touched him since she'd been in the room. Lynette listened to the monitors and watched Elijah's chest, but she had yet to reach out to him to touch him flesh to flesh. Lynette reached out her hand. It stayed suspended in midair for what seemed like infinity. But she did. She reached out and touched Elijah's arm. It was warm. Her eyes filled with tears as she leaned over.

"ELIJAH, COME BACK TO ME, PLEASE."

Lynette kissed Elijah lightly on the forehead.

"Please."

❧ 16 ❧

L ynette sat with Elijah through the night. She kept her hand on his, keeping contact with him, making sure Elijah was warm under her touch. Lynette watched the nurses come and go and checked in with each one of him to make sure Elijah's vitals said what she needed them to say. At some point, before the sun came up, Lynette closed her eyes. She intended to pray, and it started out that way. She was grateful that God spared Elijah's life and she said that. And then Lynette paused mid-prayer. There was something she didn't understand.

I know we are not supposed to question you. I know that. And God, I am asking you to forgive me for that. But I'm sad and confused. I feel like you sent Elijah to me, that he was my gift from you... that we had a divine connection and he came in my life when he did because he was a gift from you to me...because you love me. So, I don't understand why you tried to take him away from me? Unless I've been wrong this whole time and he wasn't meant for me, that Elijah isn't the one you created just for me.

She paused again as tears spilled onto her cheeks. Her eyelids trembled as she sighed.

Please let him live. Please, God let Elijah be okay. Heal him, please and restore him fully. Even if we are not meant to be and he is not my soul mate, please, let him be okay.

Amen

She paced the floor, the entire time keeping her eyes on the monitors and on Elijah. Samantha called to check in. Lynette gave her an update that there was no change. Sam asked if Lynette needed anything. She said no. They promised to talk again. She sat back down next to the bed and rested her hand on top of Elijah's. Lynette laid her head on her arm and reasoned she would just close her eyes for a few minutes. *Please, Elijah, wake up.*

She felt something. Maybe her mind was playing tricks on her. Slowly, Lynette lifted her head, and her eyes went to Elijah's hand. She needed to know if she was imaging things. And then his finger, just one, moved again. Lynette's eyes widened, and she watched to see if it happened again. His fingers twitched, and Lynette's mouth fell open. She reached over and covered his hand with hers.

"Elijah?" She whispered.

Lynette's eyes moved from Elijah's hand to his face.

Please, Elijah, wake up.

He heard his name. Elijah heard his name. He knew that voice.

She watched him intently. His lashes fluttered, and she could see his eyes moving behind his closed lids like he was trying.

"Elijah, please baby. Wake up for me, please."

There was so much peace in the quiet, but there were colors too; deep purples and light blues and a brilliant red that moved and flowed in waves across an expanse of darkness. Glints of light danced on the outskirts of the brilliant wave of colors. Elijah could easily get lost there. Yet there was another point of light; one far more brilliant than the stars that dotted the sky. His mind's eye traveled until he found that brightness, that brilliance that nearly blinded him.

Lynette
It was her smile. She was there with him under the rainbow sky. Elijah's mind went dark again, and he longed to find her. He felt a pull from her even in the darkness; he was drawn to her light. And then he heard the faintest sound of gentle water; not like a river but more like the soft sound of gentle rain. Rainbows in the sky; a precursor to rain? Then she came back to him; beads of water showering down on her, coating the ebony of her skin and washing away. Elijah saw her standing underneath that waterfall glistening like the sun. He was there with her; feeling the shower of water with her, feeling the softness of her cocoa brown skin underneath his fingertips, feeling her pull him into her, fully. She was there with him, and when he realized who it was, Lynette's face came into perfect view. The smile that captured his soul and melted his heart started to fade turning down into an arch of sadness. Her eyes were filled with despair, and it pained him. Elijah needed to see her smile again. He felt something whisper across his lips and even in the darkness of his mind, Elijah could have sworn he smelled her sweet perfume; the one that flowed from Lynette naturally. He heard his name. He felt her touch to his lips. He needed to see her smile again.

Elijah's eyes started to open. The darkness started to fade away as penetrating light pierced his orbs. Slowly, Elijah turned his head because he felt a touch. The scent of her lingered. She was there, just like she said she would be.

Lynette gripped his hand tighter and then leaned in, kissing Elijah on the forehead. She felt him; pressure against her fingers and then slowly, methodically, little by little, Lynette watched as Elijah opened his eyes.

"Hi." His voice was gruff and low, just above a whisper, but he spoke, and his eyes were open.

"Hi."

Lynette was so overwhelmed with all kinds of emotions. She reached over with both hands and placed them to the sides of Elijah's face and kissed him; pressing her lips tenderly against his forehead.

"I'm so glad you're awake and okay," Lynette whispered kissing his forehead again.

"And don't you ever scare me like that again," Lynette said lining her eyes up with his. "Promise?"

"Promise," Elijah whispered. It hurt to speak because his throat was so dry, but, Elijah ignored the pain. He needed to make the promise because he meant it.

Lynette continued to gaze into Elijah's eyes. Seeing them closed for so long, not knowing what the end result of that would be, made Lynette appreciate the beauty and the depth of Elijah's eyes even more. She felt like his soul was visible to her through them; now even more than ever. Cascades of relief wafted over Lynette, and even though she didn't intend for Elijah to see her cry, she couldn't help it. She was so grateful that he was okay.

"I thought I…" Lynette could barely bring herself to say the words aloud. Elijah saw the pain and fear in her eyes. "I thought I lost you," Lynette whimpered.

"Never," Elijah uttered, lifting his hand to make contact with her. He needed to touch Lynette as much as she needed to be touched. Feeling the warmth of her skin against his, grounded Elijah to the present. She was a beautiful reminder that he survived. Lynette blinked back the tears as much as she could despite how hard it was. She was grateful to the Creator for sparing Elijah's life. She wanted to see his survival as a kept promise from God that Elijah was indeed meant for her. The beat of Lynette's heart echoed loudly in her ears. *Don't get ahead of yourself,* Lynette secretly cautioned. *Be okay with the right now.* They shared a moment where they didn't speak. Elijah couldn't take his eyes off Lynette, and she was almost afraid to drop her gaze from him.

"I'm okay, babe," Elijah whispered. "What about Bishop?" Elijah asked, worry lines etching his face.

"He's doing okay," Lyn answered. She had been so preoccupied with worrying about Elijah she'd forgotten to mention his driver. "Lance spoke with the nurse before he and Samantha left. Bishop had some cuts and scrapes, but nothing serious," she explained. "They were going to keep him a few hours for observation."

"That's a relief," Elijah sighed. "I'm glad Samantha and Lance were here with you," Elijah rasped.

"I was a mess with them here," Lynette muttered, rolling her eyes in the top of her head. "I would have been completely in shambles if they weren't," she admitted.

"I hate I worried you, beautiful," Elijah crooned.

"You didn't do it intentionally," Lynette sighed.

"And I never will," Elijah replied.

There he goes again, Lynette thought to herself. Speaking of future as though it were real and even promised; like he saw more for them even when she was afraid to. Lynette shook her head as she stroked the side of his chiseled face.

One of the machines attached to Elijah beeped louder than it had before. Immediately Lyn's eyes shifted to the machine, and her hand fell to her heart. She looked back at Elijah to see if anything was different if he was in pain or if he was falling back into unconsciousness. He moaned, and Lynette saw Elijah's brow furrow. Lynette felt anxious as she ran her fingers through her hair. He didn't look any different to her.

"Nurse!" She screamed, turning towards the door. She reached for the call button next to Elijah and pressed the nurse button repeatedly. "Nurse!"

It wasn't long before there was a response to Lynette's outcry. A nurse came into the room. Although she was walking at a reasonable rate and responding at in a reasonable manner, Lynette felt agitated like there should have been more urgency in the nurse's response. Lynette held her tongue though. She didn't want to interfere with the nurse attending to Elijah. Lynette watched as the nurse checked the monitor. The beeping leveled off, but that didn't ally Lynette's concerns. She tracked back to Elijah. His brow was still furrowed even though he tried to unwrinkled it when he felt Lyn's eyes on him. But he was in pain and Elijah found masking his discomfort difficult. Lyn's brow furrowed in response to Elijah wincing.

"He's in pain," she urged. "Can you help him?"

The nurse offered a polite smile as she turned her attention to Elijah.

"Mr. Sinclair, I'm going to lift the sheet and check your sutures, okay?"

Elijah nodded as the nurse talked and moved at the same time. Lynette reached for Elijah's hand as the nurse attended to him. When the sheet was pulled back, and Elijah's gown was lifted Lynette saw the bandages that covered his injuries. She expected the bandages to be white, much like the sheet. But there was a tinge of blood; deep red in color, such a disturbing contrast to the whiteness of the bandage. Lynette knew better than to freak out. That would only serve to upset Elijah, and she didn't want to do that. So, she kept her response in check, doing her best to keep her eyes from widening and her mouth from gasping.

"It looks like we have a little post-surgery bleeding Mr. Sinclair," the nurse replied.

"I'm going to lift the bandage and clean the area checking to ensure the bleeding has stopped. It shouldn't hurt," the nurse continued. "But just in case I'm going to give you a sedative to ease your discomfort."

The nurse turned her attention to Lynette. "Unfortunately, the pain medication may make him sleepy."

"I understand," Lynette answered. Despite the fact that Lynette preferred Elijah awake, she much preferred him not being in pain.

Lynette watched as the nurse turned to the side table and

picked up a syringe, clicking her finger against the glass cylinder while she checked to make sure there were no bubbles in the solution. Once she was sure it was clear, the nurse inserted the needle into the IV port and depressed the plunger, releasing relief into the line. Lynette looked back at Elijah. The pained turn of his lips started to subside, and the tension in his brow started to fade. The nurse lifted the bandage and once again, Lyn's eyes were drawn to what she was doing. There was a long-jagged line of Elijah's flesh held together with stitches; dark, black thread against the mahogany of his skin. Lyn was concerned that blood would come from the wound. The nurse was careful to check each suture and to watch for more blood. She wiped away what was there, and Lynette found herself watching as well to see if more blood would appear. After a few moments, when it did not, Lyn breathed a slight sigh of relief as the nurse explained it to Elijah. His lids were heavy as he nodded just a bit.

"You should probably get some rest while he's resting," the nurse suggested as she started out of the room.

That wasn't a bad idea. Lynette hadn't slept for any significant amount of time since arriving at the hospital. How could she when the man she loved was trouble? Lynette pulled up the chair as close to the bed as she could get it. After sitting down, she looked at the monitors again just to make sure the noises coming from them were in line with what was normal. Slowly, her eyes trekked to Elijah. His eyes were inclined to her, but they were heavy with sleep.

"I'll be right here when you wake up, Lynette reassured. There was the faint smile that lingered at the corners of Elijah's lips. She reached for Elijah's hand and held it, watching until he fell asleep. Lynette took a moment after she was sure Elijah was resting peacefully to pick up her cell phone and call Samantha.

"Hey, Lyn, how's Elijah," Sam asked, picking up after the first ring.

"He woke up, Sam," Lyn whispered into the phone.

"Oh my God! That is such a relief. Bae, Elijah woke up, Samantha called to Lance." Lynette could hear Lance celebrating in the background.

"So how are you holding up, Lyn?"

"I'm yet holding," Lyn laughed trying to be light in her mood. "He had a bit of a setback, a little post operation bleeding, so the nurse came in and checked him out and gave him another sedative for the pain."

The words spilled from Lynette's lips flatly and quickly. Samantha had known Lynette for so long she could tell when something was wrong even if Lynette wouldn't admit it.

"Lynette," Samantha said.

"He's good, Sam, and I'm watching him to make sure he stays good."

"Lynette," Samantha repeated. She didn't raise her voice. There was no angst or chastisement there.

"Don't Sam, because if you call my name again, then I'll start crying and blabbering on and on about how much I love this man and almost lost him in the same breath and how God couldn't really love me because if He did, he wouldn't be doing this right now and how selfish all of this has to sound because Elijah was the one hurt. Elijah was the one in the accident, and all I can think about is how much I would lose if I lost him. So please, Sam, don't call my name again because if you do, if you say my name one more time, I'll start crying. I need to be strong for Elijah. This is not the time to be all caught up so please, don't call my name again. Don't ask me if I'm okay. Let's just focus on Elijah and that he woke up and that he's resting and that I will be here when he wakes up again. Okay? Please."

"I hear you, Lyn, I do," Samantha began. "Just remember, I'm here to be strong for you."

That statement was enough to bring tears hot and pressing

behind Lynette's eyes. She started fanning them to keep from crying.

"I'll text you guys when he wakes up again," Lynette said. It was too hard to talk. Texting would be easier. "Love you."

Samantha wasn't surprised when the line disconnected. But she knew Lyn would completely shut down if she continued to push. When Lynette was ready, she would let Sam in. Samantha would be there when she was.

Lynette put her phone on vibrate and returned it to her purse. When she turned around, Elijah was fast asleep. Lyn smiled hearing the gentle snore rumbling from his chest. She never noticed Elijah snoring before. Quietly, Lynette padded back to the chair and once again reached out for Elijah's hand. Her emotions were still all over the place; a cadre of feelings Lynette wasn't quite sure how to deal with. There was one thing, though, that Lynette knew for sure. A smile eased across her lips as she reached out gently caressing Elijah's face. Another light snore came from him, and Lynette's easy smile became a giggle. *Ah, he's so cute,* Lynette thought and then she giggled again considering that as soon as Elijah was awake, she would tease him incessantly about the snoring; of course, making it bigger than what it was. Lynette stopped giggling enough to lean in making sure there was no distance between her and Elijah. She kissed him tenderly on the lips, even as he slept.

Rest for a while, but please, wake up soon, for me.

17

"**B**eautiful," he whispered.

Awakening this time wasn't as difficult as it had been before. Things happened so quickly. One minute, Elijah was sharing a special moment with the woman that was becoming more difficult to live without. Elijah was smiling, even as he sat in the back of his chauffeur driven car, thinking about what smooth, funny, sexy thing he would say to Lynette when he called her. It had become a thing; her asking, more like strongly suggesting, that he let her know when he arrived home. It was endearing. She was attending to him; something Elijah had never had. Then next? There was a loud bang, and he was spinning not realizing the car was spinning, and then an unyielding screaming pain.

Lynette

...was his last thought, then blackness. Elijah reached for her, touching the softness of her curly tresses. The pain had subsided, and Elijah was grateful for that, but he was most grateful for Lynette being there. She was the one that drew him from the darkness. It would have been easy to give in to the pain, to just let go because there was something mystically attractive about the peace and quiet in the darkness. Peace was seductive that way. Quiet was seductive that way. A person doesn't realize how seductive calm can be because life is busy and chaotic and adrenaline-laden and exciting and wonderful until it's not because there's pain there too; and disappointment and failures that don't feel like lessons and hurt and lost love and sadness. That's when peace is attractive. And there's a light there that pulls you deeper into the peace and tranquility. There is a light there that makes you desirous of the fantasy of peace and quiet and calm and stillness. And maybe it's the Creator's peace; the idea of crossing over into eternal tranquility because that life is lulling and sweet and strong. Elijah could easily move toward that light. That peace though? That quiet and stillness and calm is also surrender. He would be leaving someone behind; someone Elijah craved, even in the midst of absolute darkness. Lynette. She was his light. The call to her essence was greater in the depths of his spirit than the desire for tranquility. The desire to spend time with her, explore her, love her, increase her was greater. Elijah had to come back to Lynette. He missed her in the stillness.

Elijah felt Lynette stir underneath his fingertips. This time, he was the one looking forward to seeing her eyes open to him. Elijah looked forward to the look in her eyes when she realized everything was going to be okay.

As she moved from sleep to awake, Lynette leaned into the feeling of Elijah's hand stroking her thick mane. She placed her hand on his, caressing his strength. Slowly, Lynette lifted her head; not wanting to lose connection with the way he made her feel.

Elijah smiled in response to the smile in Lynette's eyes when she turned to him.

"You're awake," he said winking.

"I am," Lynette smiled, "and so are you."

"I didn't want to worry you again," Elijah replied.

"I appreciate that," Lyn giggled.

"Are you thirsty, babe? Can I get you anything?"

"Water would be good," Elijah answered; still mindful of the discomfort in his throat.

Lifting Elijah's hand with her, Lynette sweetly kissed his palm as her eyes never left him. She lifted herself from the chair and padded across the room to pour Elijah a glass.

"Elijah?"

The question came just as the door started to swing open. Both Elijah and Lynette's attention were drawn to the sound and the movement.

"Mom," Elijah sighed as two distinguished figures entered the room. Even if Elijah didn't respond the way he did, it was clear that the two entering the room were his parents. Lynette took immediate note of the elegance of Mrs. Sinclair. She was statuesque, standing only a few inches shorter than her husband. The salt and pepper of her shoulder length hair beautifully framed Evelyn's face, highlighting her high cheek bones and full lips. Like a true mother, Mrs. Sinclair made a beeline straight for her son's bed. Lynette could see the etched lines of worry on her beautiful face. His father, tall and regal just like Elijah, entered the room and surveilled his surroundings, nodding to Lynette before pacing a few steps behind his wife. She could see Elijah in Mr. Sinclair; the mahogany of Ezra's skin, the shape of his nose, the broad of Mr. Sinclair's shoulders. Mrs. Sinclair dropped her designer bag and lifted her son's hand to her chestnut brown face in one motion.

"I was so worried about you," Evelyn whispered taking in the fullness of her son through hooded eyes.

"I'm fine, mom, really," Elijah explain receiving the loving kiss Evelyn planted on his cheek.

"Good to see you're doing okay, son," Mr. Sinclair said as his wife took a step to the side so Elijah's father could greet him. The handshake often shared between men was not what occurred when Mr. Sinclair greeted his son. Instead, Ezra lowered his frame and placed his forehead against his sons. They didn't share words at that moment, but it was clear, even from where Lyn stood, that they connected. As Mr. Sinclair stood up, he again turned in Lynette's direction.

"Forgive our rudeness," Mr. Sinclair began.

"No need," Lynette smiled. "I understand."

"Mom, dad, this is Lynette Jones."

"Very nice to meet you, Ms. Jones," Mr. Sinclair smiled, extending his hand and politely shaking Lynette's.

"Thank you for being here with our son," Mrs. Sinclair offered.

"It's the least I can do," Lynette replied. Taking a step forward, Lynette extended the glass to Elijah and waited until he took a few sips before returning the glass to the table beside him.

"I'll step out of the room so you and your parents can visit," Lynette smiled.

Before Elijah could raise his objection, his mother spoke.

"You don't have to do that," Mrs. Sinclair interjected.

"No, it's fine, ma'am," Lynette answered. "You all have come a long way to see him," she smiled. "I'll see you in a little while."

Elijah nodded his head and watched as Lynette exited the room.

"Son, what happened," Mr. Sinclair inquired.

"We got a call from Lance, Mrs. Sinclair added. "All I heard was accident and hospital. I couldn't focus on anything else."

"Apparently, a driver ran through a stoplight and broadsided the car," Elijah explained.

"Were you able to get the other driver's information," Mr. Sinclair asked. Elijah was aware that his father was going with that line of questioning. Ezra would ensure that whoever was responsible for hurting his son took full responsibility for their actions.

"I wasn't in a position to, but I'm sure the police did," Elijah answered.

Mr. Sinclair made a mental note to follow up on the matter. He didn't want to belabor the point considering the most important thing was the health and safety of his son. However, Ezra intended to handle the situation.

"How bad were you hurt?" Evelyn pressed, still carrying some physical signs of worry.

"Enough to require surgery," Elijah answered. "But I should fully recover."

"With God's grace," Evelyn sighed. Neither Ezra nor Evelyn were overly religious. Elijah knew his parents to be spiritual though; recognizing that there was a higher power, one who guided our individual affairs. Evelyn adjusted in her chair before continuing.

"There's a little bit more to it than just Ms. Jones," Evelyn quipped as she took the seat next to Elijah's bed. "Don't you think so, Ezra?"

"Sounds like it to me," Mr. Sinclair agreed.

"Mom, really?" Elijah sighed. "You just got here and already?"

He couldn't do anything but shake his head and chuckle behind his mother's comment. Elijah was not surprised in the least.

"I have raised respectable, accomplished sons," Evelyn went on. "That's not being braggadocious. Those are merely the facts. Now, I need them to find their better halves, so I can have grandchildren to spoil."

Mr. Sinclair and Elijah shared a knowing gaze.

"Because you in no way spoiled our boys," Mr. Sinclair bantered. Elijah chuckled watching the exchange between his parents.

"Of course not," Evelyn corrected.

"Well, that's a matter of interpretation," Ezra continued, striding across the room and taking up residence on the couch across from Elijah's bed. "Don't you agree, son?"

"Oh, no," Elijah rebuffed. Lifting both his hands in surrender. "I refuse to get in the middle of that one."

"It wouldn't matter if you did," Evelyn smiled. "Besides, the only interpretation that truly matters is mine," she laughed.

"A mess," Elijah chuckled.

"But you love me," Evelyn laughed again. She felt better seeing that her son was okay. Although she minimized her reaction to the news that Elijah was in an accident, Evelyn panicked, fearing the worst. She couldn't settle until she saw with her own eyes that her son was indeed okay. Lance had been a wonderful friend, doing his best to reassure them that Elijah was okay. Lance even called to update them when Elijah woke up. Evelyn appreciated knowing, but it wasn't the same as seeing for herself. Seeing Elijah alert, hearing his voice, seeing his smile was enough. Evelyn could breathe again.

Lynette took the time away from Elijah to step outside of the hospital to get some fresh air. The pace in which she exited the hospital was very different than the pace in which she entered. But the feeling of worry, angst, and anxiety rushing into the unknown was felt as she passed through the automated doors again. Lynette slightly lifted her head as she inhaled the newness of the air around her. The warmth of the sun's rays felt good on her skin. The afternoon Atlanta sky was bright with billowy clouds that stealthily moved across the wide expanse. As Lynette meandered along the walkway, she took note of the newness of the day. Finding an unoccupied bench, Lynette sat down and breathed in deeply. There were others along the walkway, families, couples, patients; some in wheelchairs, others attached to equipment that undoubtedly helped them stay alive. These were not things Lynette never saw before. Like most people, she had. Yet, having someone close to you go through a thing brought on a new level of appreciation for things we so often take for granted. Although Elijah may not be completely out of the woods, Lyn appreciated where he was. She took a moment to say just how she felt.

Gracious Heavenly Father, thank you for your mercy and your kindness. Thank you for bringing Elijah back to me. Thank you for protecting him. Lynette paused as she stroked the back of Elijah's hand, tracing her thumb against him. *And God if he is not the man you designed for me, steel my heart, Lord, please. Build me up so I won't break if he is not the one; my one. I ask these things in your name amen.*

By the time Lynette reentered the hospital, she felt refreshed. There was a spring in her step that hadn't been there before. And in some ways, despite lingering trepidation, she felt some peace as she rode the elevator back to the third floor. Upon arriving at Elijah's room, Lynette rapped lightly on Elijah's door before entering.

"Come in," a familiar voice called out. Lynette was glad to see that the mood was light when she reentered the space. The family was engaged in lively conversation, and there was laughter that could be heard outside the door. Elijah was awake and smiling as Lyn sauntered across the room.

"We were just talking about you," Mrs. Sinclair said as Lynette rounded the foot of Elijah's bed.

Her brow slightly raised hearing she was the subject of conversation.

"I hope in a good way," Lynette nervously smiled. She felt her cheeks flush warmly as the nervous smile stretched across her full lips.

"In the best possible way," Elijah crooned, reaching for her hand. "I missed you," he whispered at a pitch Lynette was sure his parents heard. Folding her hand into his, Lynette mouthed, 'I missed you, too.'

"We may be old, but our hearing is still pretty good," Mr. Sinclair chortled.

"Who are you calling old, honey," Evelyn sassed. Lynette, dear, he is speaking for himself talking like that," Evelyn corrected.

"Don't hold my parents against me," Elijah teased as his parents continued to banter back and forth.

"I like them," Lynette replied, leaning down and speaking directly into Elijah's ear. "So, what did they say about me, Lynette asked, being careful not to be rude by having a separate conversation.

"That you are the best thing that's ever happened to me," Elijah crooned. Much of the smoothness of Elijah's voice had returned. He didn't seem to be struggling as much to speak.

She pulled back to look Elijah in the face. He smiled at the suspicious turn of her lips like she didn't believe what he said. He smirked and his brow lifted.

"Oh, so you don't believe me," Elijah challenged. Before Lynette could respond, Elijah cleared his throat.

"Excuse me, mom, dad," he began. Even before he said anything more, Lynette's eyes widened, and she playfully swatted his arm in an effort to deter whatever was next. Feeling his parents' eyes on her, Lynette smiled and then turned and threatened Elijah through tightly clenched teeth.

"Don't," she hissed.

Elijah smiled even more and once he gained his parents' full attention carried on as if the threat didn't exist.

"Lyn is curious to know what was said about her."

"No, really, I'm not," Lynette quickly inserted.

"I don't know why not," Evelyn replied. "It was all good."

Prickly heat treading up Lynette's cheeks was hard to contain.

"Whatever it was, thank you, Lynette smiled.

"I told her you all said she was the best thing that ever happened to me," Elijah repeated.

"True," Mr. Sinclair chimed in. "It's written all over my son's face; how he watched you leave the room and how he beamed when you came in."

"Reminds me of someone I know," Evelyn taunted. Mr. Sinclair knew a compliment when he heard one. It only took a few long strides before he was next to his wife, leaning over and kissing her.

"Don't start," Elijah moaned embarrassedly.

"Leave your parents alone," Lynette chided. "They're adorable."

And they were. Lynette could see his parents influence on the way Elijah treated her the way he attended to her, the way he showed how much he cared about her. Elijah had a wonderful example in the love shown by his parents.

18

TWO WEEKS LATER

Lynette and Elijah spent every moment they could together after his hospitalization. Although neither of them said it aloud, it was as though their subconscious was in agreement that time spent apart was wasted time. Lance had been a wonderful boss during this time; giving Lyn time off to take care of Elijah, especially after his parents returned home.

"How are you feeling, babe," Lynette asked as they lay snuggled in Elijah's bed.

"Good, beautiful," Elijah replied strummed. "The doctor gave me the all clear to fully resume my regular duties." With a wink and a sexy smile, Elijah put his arm around Lyn's waist and caressed her affectionately.

"Don't be getting no ideas, Mr. Sinclair," Lynette purred.

"Too late," Elijah moaned, tracing his fingers delicately across Lynette's thighs. She couldn't help the moan that passed through her lips. Elijah had that kind of effect on her.

"Stop, babe," you just got out of the hospital," Lynette rebuffed even though her body yearned for more. Elijah looked her over seductively as his manhood responded to her nearness. He radiated such vitality, Lynette could hardly resist.

"Full duties," Elijah hummed tracing his fingers even higher on her thighs, teasing her erogenous zone.

"I know what the doctor said," Lynette panted. "But I don't want to hurt you."

Reaching for her hand, Elijah captured it in his own and guided it against his flesh. Lynette's pulse skittered alarmingly as Elijah guided her hand to his pulsating thickness. A delightful shiver of wanting danced through her, as Lyn felt his dick rising to meet her touch.

"Full duties," he moaned as the energy from her touch coursed through him, awakening the licentious beast within.

This time Elijah's caress was more a demand. Their closeness was like an intoxicating drug to Lynette lulling her into anticipated euphoria. Lifting from the bed, Lynette gently straddled Elijah. She was mindful of his injury, but his thoughts were not there. His dick thumped hard as his hands found the curve of her waist. Planting her feet on each side of him, Lynette lifted his thickness to her; the fold of her pussy lips enveloping his throbbing tip and welcoming him in.

"Sss," she purred as her womanly flesh melded and contorted to take his engorged shaft in. Hearing the guttural moan from Elijah as he entered her, drove Lynette to the brink. He lifted to reach the top of her yoni as Lynette lowered herself taking him in to the hilt. Her grind on Elijah's cock was slow, circular and then counterclockwise so he could feel every facet of her jewel.

"Bae damn," Elijah rasped in a husky whisper.

"Elijah," Lynette sang as he filled her to capacity. Her slow grind became a rhythmic bounce as the first wave of scintillating climax moved through her, giving Elijah the first taste of wetness that coated his dick. Lyn's head fell back between her shoulder blades as Elijah gripped her waist tighter. They were in perfect sync and the sound of Lyn's ass slapping against Elijah's thighs propelled them into a faster fuck.

"Oh, babe," Lyn panted as her full breasts bounced from

the fuck he was giving her. He missed her. Elijah's body missed her, and he needed to remind Lynette that he was there, present, willing and ready to love her in every possible way. Lifting his torso from the bed, Elijah wrapped his strong arms arounds Lyn's waist. Her head inclined to him and their eyes met, and Elijah's eyes told Lynette everything she needed to know. She felt it pulse through her, eradicating her doubts and allying any fears.

His eyes were possessive and claiming. They spoke his reassurance and promise to her. A new wave of pulsating energy moved through Lynette as Elijah pleased her mentally physically and soulfully.

"Ah, ah, ah," she panted. Elijah's body convulsed as a stream of gism pressed for release.

"Together?" Lyn asked, feeling the same kind of pressing in her puss.

"Together," Elijah groaned as their bodies rocketed from the electrifying orgasm exploding between them.

Two Weeks later

IT WAS near the end of Lynette' shift. The mailroom had been exceptionally busy throughout the day and Lynette was ready for it to be over. Her work area was clear, and all Lyn had left was to finish her final tabulations for the day. She was already thinking forward to her time with Elijah.

"Excuse me," one of the mailroom runners said as he sat three boxes on Lynette's station.

"Hold up, excuse me," Lyn insisted catching the young man's attention before he walked away. She had to reach out and tap the runner on the shoulder to gain his full attention as he wore earbuds in his ears.

"Oh, sorry about that," the runner apologized.

"Where did these packages come from," Lynette inquired; sliding her hand over her hip and leaning into it.

"I don't know ma'am," the runner explained. "I was just told to bring them to the mailroom.

"Do you know what time it is?"

Shrugging his shoulders, the young man looked up at the wall on the clock and then back at Lynette. Before he could even open her mouth, Lyn threw up her hand halting any further commentary from the young fellow.

"Listen, you go back and tell your boss, whoever that is, that last mail deliveries are accepted up until 4:30 p.m. East Standard Pacific time and not one minute later. Do you understand?"

"Yes ma'am," the runner smiled, tipping the bib of his hat. Lyn watched as the young man eased his buds back into his ears and rhythmically walked away, bopping to a beat only he could hear.

She looked around to see if any of the other sorters were still on the floor.

"Tsk," she popped her lips, realizing she was the only one. She sighed deeply, her shoulders lifting and falling. Her coworkers had been good to Lyn when she needed the time off so Lynette decided she would take this one for the team.

"Let's see what we have here" Lynette murmured as she

lifted the first package. Even before reading the label to see what mail bin to sort the package to, Lynette took note of the paper the box was wrapped in.

"Oui, oui, Paris," Lynette hummed seeing the faint Eifel Towers embossed on the wrapping. She stopped short as her eyes traveled across the label and she read her own name, destination, mailroom.

"Wha-," Lyn paused unable to finish her thought. She was befuddled. Her eyes trekked cross the label again. There it was her name Lynette Jones, followed by destination, mailroom. But that made it seem like it was an internal package not one received from outside. There was no return label and upon closer inspection there was no stamp indicating where the package came from. Lynette's brow was furrowed as she looked around the mailroom. She was still the only one there.

Her hands were slow in moving as she traced the shape of the box with both hands before deciding to open it. Lynette peeled the tape from the paper, being careful not to rip it; just the opposite of a child on Christmas morning ripping the wrapping paper to shreds. Sitting the wrapping paper to the side, Lynette opened the box that was inside. She folded down one corner of the box then the next until all four sides of the box were opened. There was a slight tilt to Lynette's head as she looked inside the box and then carefully lifted out an envelope addressed to her. Even though curiosity was getting the best of Lyn, she still was quick to move. She proceeded with caution as she lifted the lip on the envelope and pulled out the handwritten letter.

"*Beautiful*," Lynette's heart instantly dropped. There was only one person who called her beautiful.

Do you remember when I asked you to tell me your fantasies about the places you could only dream of going?

"Read it aloud," a strong sexy voice sounded from behind her. A quake moved through her and Lynette's knees felt weak. She knew that voice. Lynette loved that voice. Yet, she couldn't respond to that voice. Her heart bounded in her chest. There was a knot in her stomach. Lynette heard his footfalls behind her. Elijah's strides were purposeful.

"Read it out loud," Elijah encouraged, standing immediately behind Lynette' close enough for her to feel his physical presence. He noticed Lyn's shoulders shivering and placed a firm hand to the center of her back. Her inhale was audible as Elijah's touch was magical. With a tremor in her hand Lyn lifted the paper.

"I want," Lynette started to read but her eyes had clouded over with tears making it difficult. Elijah turned Lynette in his hands so he could see her face and she could see his.

"I want to make every single one of your fantasies come true," Elijah continued as though reading from the paper. Lynette's eyes fluttered shut and the first tear fell to her cheek.

"There is something about uncertainty that makes you certain," Elijah continued. "I love you, beautiful. I am in love with you. Before the accident I knew that I wanted to spend the rest of my life with you, and that's still true. But now, I can't wait a respectable amount of time to ask you to be my wife. Now, I can't propose and then wait six, ten, twelve months for the right season for us to get married. There is something about certainty that makes you certain. Lynette, I need you to marry me. I need you to say yes so you can be my wife. I need you to say yes so I can make those fantasies come true right away."

He turned Lynette around again so she could see the table.

"Each one of those boxes represents the places you fantasized about traveling to. You told me you fantasized about going to Paris because of the romance. When you say yes, we'll spend our honeymoon there. When you mentioned you fantasized about traveling to Africa, to the motherland, to where it all started, we'll go there, too beloved, and visit the tree I had planted for you there. When you mentioned wanting to go to the Caribbean, it was because of the turquoise water and the white sandy beaches. When you say yes, we'll walk hand in hand along the beach in front of the house I'll build for you there."

This time when Elijah helped Lynette to turn around, they were no longer the only two people in the room. Behind Elijah was Lace and Samantha and her coworkers from the mailroom. Lynette was so overcome by the outpouring of love she felt from Elijah that was echoed in the faces of her friends, she found it hard to breathe. Her hand went to her chest covering her heart. She could feel the pounding through her fingers. For Lynette it felt like there was no air left in her lungs to gasp when Elijah dropped to one knee.

"Lynette, uncertainty makes you certain about some things. And I am certain about you." Elijah removed a small box from his pocket and opened it. "Beautiful will you marry me?"

Lyn didn't even see the five-carat pear shaped diamond in the velvet box. Her head nodded before her mouth opened. "Yes, yes, oh my God, Elijah yes!"

Lynette reached for Elijah wrapping her arms tightly around his neck as he stood to his feet. "Yes, babe, yes I will marry you," she cried against his cheek.

A cheer erupted from the friends that were gathered around. Samantha wiped a tear from her eye as she watched Lynette and Elijah. "Yes," Samantha uttered. "She said yes."

19

ONE MONTH LATER

The location of the wedding was a nod to Elijah's architectural accoutrement and his love for beautifully orchestrated structures; particularly second renaissance revival style architecture. Sitting atop a hill and built in 1928, the classically historic Swan House, the iconic mansion was home to several exquisite venues both indoors and outdoors, offering luxurious surroundings and made for the perfect backdrop to Elijah and Lynette's big day. The Grand Overlook Ballroom featuring a stone barreled ceiling, Brazilian cherry wood floors and a picture -perfect view of the woody, illuminated Quarry Garden was filled with one hundred of Elijah and Lynette's closest friends and family. Their parents were seated on the first row, Evelyn and Ezra on one side, and Lynette's mother, Cynthia across from them. Lyn's father, Vincent stood nervously in the hallway of the mansion awaiting his baby girl's arrival.

"I can't believe this is really happening," Lynette uttered as she sat in the bridal suite with her best friend. "Not too long ago I was your maid of honor, and now," Lynette paused.

"And now, I'm your matron of honor," Samantha sang as she adjusted the hem of her matron's gown; a floor length ensemble in pale yellow with a beaded bodice and heart shaped neckline. Both Lyn and Sam's gown were custom designs by African American wedding designer, Me Jeanne Couture.

The make-up artist put the finishing touches on Lynette's understated but elegant look and then it was time for Lynette to put on her dress.

"That gown is amazing," Samantha mused as Lynette lifted herself from the make-up chair and gently padded across the bridal suite. "Let me help you," Sam suggested as she followed Lyn to the other side of the room. Me Jeanne had done a magnificent job on the customized gown; a shimmering white, single shoulder floor length gown. The bodice was emblazoned with Swarovski crystals under sheer lace and the tulle skirt flared nicely from the curve of Samantha's hips. Lynette's hair was upswept, with loose curls framing her face, reminiscent of the night she met Elijah. The simple but elegant diamond stud earrings played nicely against the elegant simplicity of her gown. Samantha eased the zipper to its final resting place and handed Lyn her bridal bouquet; pale yellow roses highlighted with crystal embellishments throughout the bouquet. Lyn saw herself reflected in the floor length mirror nearby. Her eyes traveled the length of her reflection. She had been transformed in so many ways. She entered the suite a woman in love, and now looking upon herself, Lynette was a bride.

"I am so happy for you, Lyn," Sam suggested as she peered over her friend's shoulder and saw how beautiful Lynette looked.

"Thank you, Sam," Lynette answered pivoting around and giving Sam a hug. "None of this would have been possible without you."

"I wouldn't say that," Sam smiled. "I think Elijah may have had a little something to do with it," Samantha teased. I'll see you out there, okay?"

Lynette nodded smilingly, "okay."

With one final look in the mirror, Lynette was ready to see her soon-to-be-husband. As she exited the suite, an usher was there to assist Lynette in navigating down the long hallway. Surprisingly, Lynette didn't feel nervous or anxious as she made her way to the ballroom. She was excited to see Elijah and even more excited to know that she was marrying the man of her dreams.

"Lynny poo," Lyn's father sighed as his daughter approached. Lynn could see it in her father's eyes. he was proud of her and desperately afraid of losing her, all at the same time.

"I will always be your Lynny poo," Lynette smiled, lifting onto her tiptoes and kissing her father on the cheek.

"You better," Vincent strummed. "Shall we?"

Lyn's dad extended his arm and Lynette dutifully laced her arm around his.

"We shall."

As they approached the French doors to the ballroom, Vincent looked down at his daughter one last time. Lynette had always been his baby girl. When those doors opened, he would walk down the aisle and give her away. Although symbolic and traditional, it wasn't going to be easy for Vincent. But Vince would do it because his daughter deserved every happiness. Vince would do it because he knew Elijah made Lyn happy.

The four-piece string quartet began to play as the French doors were opened. Friends and family greeted Lyn as she made her way down the rose petal covered aisle. She smiled as she recognized the song the quartet played and found herself humming the lyrics in her head as she made her way to Elijah. *Sparkle in your eye, sparkle in your eye*, Lynette hummed. *When I look at you, dreams do come true...*

And there he was Elijah, waiting there to receive her. Lynette smiled again. Elijah looked just as good coming as he did going, and he looked strikingly handsome in the Bottega Venetta single-breasted custom tuxedo he wore.

"Family and friends, we are gathered here today to celebrate a truly special occasion; the union of Ms. Lynette Jones and Mr. Elijah Sinclair. I know you've heard it before, but a union of this level is not to be entered into lightly. This is a sacred union, a trust bond that connects the minds hearts and souls of two people that love each other." The minister paused. "Who give this woman to be wed?"

"My wife and I do," Vincent answered boldly. Elijah strode towards Lynette and her father, firmly shaking Mr. Jones' hand before accepting Lyn's; taking her arm with gentle authority.

"Thank you, sir," Elijah said.

Vince nodded his head, again giving his approval of their union. Elijah had been respectful enough and man enough to ask for Lynette's hand in marriage before proposing to Lyn. Vincent respected that and was honored by the deference Elijah showed. Elijah's touch against her hand was like the first time he touched her; thrilling, intense yet soothing all in one. Lance stood as Elijah's best man and Samantha stood as Lyn's matron.

Now, I don't know about you, but I can see the love these two people share. I feel the amorous vibration emanating between them. I sense the depths of their connectedness."

The minister paused before continuing, allowing his words to be absorbed and the couple to be appreciated.

"Those of us here sharing in this ceremony with Elijah and Lynette have a responsibility to this couple. You were invited as a witness to the sacred vows they will soon make to each other. As witnesses, it is our responsibility to encourage Elijah and Lynette to hold their vows close to their hearts, to honor their partner in all that they do, and be mindful of their partner in all things. Do you agree, as a witness to this coming together, to support Elijah and Lynette in their love for each other? If it is true for you, please respond with I do."

There was a chorused response from the audience of, "I do."

"Elijah, Lynette, I understand you have written your own vows?"

The bride and groom nodded in response to the minister's inquiry.

"Well, Elijah, speak your heart to Lynette."

As he had done so many times in the past, Elijah caressed Lynette's hands as he held them. She felt like she couldn't breathe. This was all so surreal. Elijah's unwavering gaze into Lynette's eyes was a beautiful reminder that he was in fact real, and his words echoed the same.

"Beloved, I have been a man on a mission since the first time I saw you. I knew then that there was something extraordinary about you and I was determined to find out what that something was. And I did. You have a smile that was meant to brighten even my darkest day. You have so much compassion that it causes me to be more compassionate. Your beauty emanates from within and spills out into this amazingly beautiful woman I see before me. I thank the Creator for you. Lynette, you have a heart that was made to love me, just me, and I'm eternally grateful. And I promise to forever appreciate you, honor you, respect you, uphold you, be strength for you and cherish you. When the doctors weren't sure I would recover, when there were lingering questions in my own mind as to whether I would pull through, it was you who reminded me what light was and compelled me out of the darkness. You kissed me back to life, beloved."

"My dearest Elijah, you came to me at a time in my life when I wasn't sure true love would ever find me. I learned to be happy for others who did find the love they desired. I wasn't even sure I deserved the kind of love that I only found in my dreams. But you dispelled all of that for me. You showed me with your actions and reminded me with your words that real love was meant for me; that I too could have the kind of unconditional, earth shattering love that I secretly craved. Even more than that, you insisted that I know I deserved that kind of love. I love you with my whole heart. You make it so easy," Lynette smiled.

"And just as you reminded me that love was possible, it's my turn to remind you that my heart beats for you; that this love I have in my heart, that unconditional, devoted earth-shattering love is reserved just for you. With all my heart, I promise to honor you as the incredible man I know you to be. I promise to support you as the head of our family because you are a man with vision for our future. I promise to lean in when you need me even if you don't say it. And I promise to cherish every single moment I have with you. It was you, Elijah Sinclair, who kissed me back to life, and for that I will forever be grateful."

The swoon that moved through the room was heard and felt by all. Samantha dabbed lightly at the tears threatening to spill onto her cheeks. Sam couldn't be happier for Lynette. She knew the struggle, the late nights of WWE, and how Lynette settled for being just okay. To see her best friend so in love and so happy, made it difficult to keep from crying.

"When lovers speak from their heart you know it, you feel it and you believe it," the minister replied. "Elijah and Lynette have shared their vows, have given and exchanged the rings sealing their declaration of love to the world," the minister continued. "There's only one thing left to do."

Elijah smiled as he felt Lynette vibrating through their joined hands. Her eyes were bright, and her smile was wide, and she was ready for the pronouncement. The minister noticed it, too. Lyn was literally shaking with excitement.

"Elijah, you may kiss your bride."

Elijah guided Lynette into him, first with his eyes and then with a gently pull which Lyn readily gave into. He felt the vibration pulse through her and penetrate his essence as their lips joined in a heated kiss. In that moment, Lynette and Elijah were the only two people in the world; their singular orbits merged transcendentally in a space reserved just for them. But they were not alone and the ooh's and aah's and outpouring of love from the audience behind the couple's tantalizing kiss, said so.

"Ladies and gentlemen, it is my distinct pleasure to present for the first time, Mr. and Mrs. Elijah and Lynette Sinclair!"

The audience stood to their feet as the presentation of the new couple was made. Lynette was smitten all over again, knowing that the man standing next to her, holding her hand and leveling her with a powerfully intense gaze was now her husband. Elijah must have felt just as consumed by the over-whelming joy and happiness he felt, so much so that pulled Lynette in dipping her low with the strength of his arms as his lips came coaxingly down on hers smothering Lyn's lips with demanding mastery. Lynette felt her knees buckle as she succumbed to the pressing of his mouth to hers.

"Whew chile," someone from the audience exclaimed as Elijah eased his bride to her feet. The two remained locked in a scintillating gaze as the audience cheered. Taking her hand once again into his own, Elijah and Lynette proceeded down the aisle and out of the historic hall into the early evening air. They were showered with multicolored flower petals as they walked down the stairs to the car waiting for them.

"Oh my God, Candy!" Lynette happily exclaimed as she saw the 1950 candy apple red four door Chevy Deluxe Hot Rod Coupe donning a big silver bow. Reaching into the pocket of his tuxedo pants, Elijah pulled out a key and placed it in Lynette's hand.

"She's all yours," he chortled.

"Baby, what?" Lynette gasped. "You're giving Candy to me?"

Elijah nodded. "Babe," Lynette squealed, throwing her arms around Elijah's neck.

"You are just too good to me babe," she whispered causing a sexy smile to dance on the corners of his lips.

"Always," Elijah muttered against the warmth of her neck.

"I'm driving," Lynette laughed as she stepped away from Elijah and dangled her new key in the air. As the two made their way over to Candy, Bishop was there to open the driver side door for Lynette.

"Thank you, Bishop," Lynette winked as she slid into the driver's seat.

"My pleasure, Mrs. Sinclair," Bishop smiled.

Elijah eased his frame into the passenger seat and closed the door.

"Are you ready, beloved?"

"To spend the rest of my life with you? Absolutely!" Lynette gushed. Turning the key over in the ignition, Lynette beamed as she heard the smooth purr of Candy powering to life. Lynette's smile was infectious as she put the Chevy Coupe in gear; the two of them, riding off into the sunset together.

The End

THANK you so much for reading Lynette and Elijah's story. I would really appreciate it, especially if you enjoyed the story, to leave a review on Amazon and Goodreads. For Indie authors, reviews are the lifeblood of our work. They give other readers insight into the story and greater visibility for the authors. Thanks in advance and I hope you will continue reading the Moore Friends Series with me!

If you haven't already, please check out,
Other Books Written by Celeste:

All That & Moore Series:
Hidden Missing Moore
I Am Moore
Teach Me Moore
Expect Moore
So Much Moore
Never Moore
I Found Moore

MOORE TO LOVE SERIES:
Stipulations
Gabriel's Melody
Temptations

MOORE FRIENDS SERIES:
Something New
Before I Fall
Lady Guardians Series:
Onyx Rides
Cruisin'

Coming Soon!

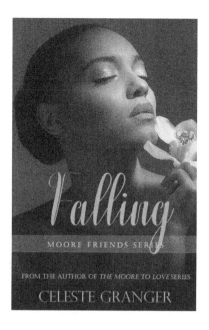

Want to be in the know? Subscribe to my newsletter to be a part of Celeste Granger's Tangled Romance!

HTTPS://LANDING.MAILERLITE.COM/WEBFORMS/LANDING/K2E1J4

Join my Reading Group! https://www.facebook.com/groups/1943300475969127/

Follow me on Facebook @ https://www.facebook.com/TheCelesteGranger/

Made in the USA
Middletown, DE
22 April 2025

74623838R00096